I0550596

Kerry Mc Daniels's Quest

By: Jeanne Taylor Thomas

Copyright 2012

Kerry McDaniels Quest

All Rights Reserved

Copyright 2012 Jeanne Taylor Thomas

Cover design 2012 Rae Monet, Inc. All rights reserved – used with permission.

Discover other titles by Jeanne Taylor Thomas at jeannetaylorthomas.com

This is a work of fiction. The events and characters described herein are imaginary and are not intended to refer to specific places or living persons. The opinions expressed in this manuscript are solely the opinions of the author and do not represent the opinions or thoughts of the publisher. The author has represented and warranted full ownership and/or legal right to publish all the materials in this book.

All characters in this book have no existence outside the imagination of the author and have no relation whatsoever to anyone bearing the same name or names. They are not even distantly inspired by any individual know or unknown to the author and all incidents are pure invention.

This book may not be reproduced, transmitted, or stored in whole or in part by any means, including graphic, electronic, or mechanical without the express written consent of the author except in the case of brief quotations embodied in critical articles and reviews.

ISBN: 978-0615736921

PRINTED IN THE UNITED STATES OF AMERICA

ACKNOWLEDGEMENTS

Without the help and support from the following, this book would never have come to life.

I thank Kerry Thomas, Cass Abbott, Doree Anderson, Jewels Coleman, Richard Palazzolo and Madelyn Peters for their time and suggestion.

This book is dedicated To
My wonderful mother, Donna Taylor
For all of your love and Encouragement

Kerry McDaniels Quest

Shawgun, the demon skin walker, is in pursuit of Kerry to acquire back his claw, the only thing holding him in this realm. Using his powers, he manipulates others to kill Kerry, because killing Kerry himself would leave the power of the claw useless.

Nakiya is caught in the trap Shawgun set, and Kerry's emotions work against him. Can he learn to control those emotions before he destroys himself and Moon Dancer, as Moon Dancer grows weaker each time Kerry's focus deviates from their mission.

Prologue

Two months ago I found out I shared my soul with an ancient Blackfeet Indian Shaman, Moon Dancer. My soul wasn't all we shared under this curse. Moon Dancer also shared my mind and that had taken some getting used to. I was always checking to make sure it was me, Kerry McDaniels, inside these shirts and blue jeans. Once before we'd used Moon Dancer's body from his youth and it was a weird experience to say the least while we searched the planet Icebis for one of his stolen gifts.

Moon Dancer had special gifts stolen from him by Shawgun an evil demon skin-walker. Those stolen gifts we had to find in order to separate our souls. Shawgun had attempted to stop Moon Dancer from being born again as punishment for stopping him from using Moon Dancer's sister for a blood sacrifice.

We found one of Moon Dancer's gifts, 'animal spirits, the gift to keep part of an animal's spirit when it passed from this world,' on the planet Icebis. Our recovery of that gift set Shawgun on a raging killing rampage. Shawgun had lost his ability to teleport himself to Icebis and was bound to this plane of the universe.

When Shadow and I found the cave I started to have dreams. Each dream had sent Shawgun, an evil skin-walker demon on a killing spree, shape shifting into a grizzly bear. Shawgun lost a claw when he was shot by a ranch hand. That claw now hung from my neck and was the only protection that kept me safe from the demon skin-walker. That power in the claw had to be gifted back to Shawgun. If Shawgun killed me for the claw, it would render the rest of his power useless. I didn't know who made up the ancient rules, but I was glad for that one.

I'd said my goodbyes' to Nakiya and her brother Josh, Moon Dancer's great- great- grandchildren, whom the demon also hunted. They had left Montana to go back to Tennessee with their parents taking a load of horses back to their ranch. Nakiya had captured my heart and it had been hard to say goodbye. The only good thing I knew for sure was she and Josh would be back at our ranch for Christmas.

Shawgun had tried to use Nakiya against me but at the time I didn't have the claw as he had hoped to make an exchange. With Josh and Nakiya both gone back to Tennessee that gave me more time to learn how to use the gift we found on the planet Icebis. I'd accidently swallowed the small globe when we found it, so now I had to learn to control my own shape shifting.

With me leaving for Havre to go to taxidermy school and Nakiya and Josh on their way to Tennessee I hoped the killing would stop. My parents along with other ranchers had lost enough money on killed livestock due to my dreams. I was walking the razor's edge between two worlds and my life would never be the same.

CHAPTER ONE

Glancing around my bedroom, I set the second suitcase down next to the other one by the door. I grabbed my train tickets and tucked them into the side of my camera bag. In a few hours I'll be on my way to taxidermy school in Havre, Montana. The last thing to do was put a snack together for my train ride.

As I entered the kitchen, Mom was bustling around making breakfast. I sat up at the counter.

"I'll leave it up to you to decide what you want to take for your snack," Mom said, putting her arm around my shoulder, she gave me a hug. Sitting up on the bar stool next to me her sky blue eyes glistened. Her smile didn't have the radiance I was used to seeing on her face.

On the counter were four different kinds of cookies, along with honey balls, cinnamon rolls, peanut brittle and fudge.

"You can tell who gets spoiled around here," Steve said jokingly, one of my older brothers, coming through the kitchen door followed by my brothers Jace and Rob. My brothers were all tall and muscular with various shades of brownish-red hair, and we all had Mom and Dad's color of blue eyes. My brothers and I were close and even though we all had different work load on the ranch we helped each other when it was needed. My dad trailed them and the screen door closed behind him with a resounding smack.

"Wow, smells delicious Sally," Dad said to Mom. "Don't tell me it's all for Kerry. If he eats all that, the school will send him back because the doorways won't accommodate him!" He gave Mom a kiss on the cheek.

"When did you get back, Steve?" I asked, shaking his hand and then pulling him in for a hug.

"This morning, I've been out with Dad and Rob talking to the ranchers about that rogue bear."

I glanced over at Jace, and finished packing my goodies. That rogue bear they were talking about was the demon, Shawgun.

When I had returned from the powwow, I'd confided only in Jace, my brother three years older than I, about the demon and the connection with my dreams. With every dream I had in the cave, Shawgun had killed cattle not only on our ranch but on other ranches in the area. Jace, being the county veterinarian (after Doc Hammond passed away) had seen the cattle mutilated by Shawgun.

"So, what did you come up with?" I asked, not looking up.

"Well, Jace doesn't want to set more traps," said Steve. "He's afraid of hurting or killing other animals. The foremen on Ross Stevens and Andy Holdenson's ranches and some of the neighboring ranchers want to take out a hunting party." Our ranches were spread wide apart though out the county, however if there was trouble we banded together to help each other.

"Since we haven't seen any tracks, they don't know where to begin, and with the roundup in ten days, they really need all their hands for that." My brother sighed, and picked up a cinnamon roll.

"Doesn't help that the Ross Stevens' ranch hand keeps ranting about that bear, saying he's a demon bear; a skin walker," Rob added, as he scooped up a chocolate chip cookie.

"A skin walker? Where would he come up with something like that?" The muscles surrounding my chest tightened, but I still forced a disbelieving chuckle. "I thought skin walkers were only found in the southwest?" Skin-walkers were known to be demons in an animal's skin. They were evil and could make others do their bidding and some even did human sacrifice. Like the Navajo Skin walker that was going to sacrifice Moon Dancer's sister, Spotted Fawn.

"The ranch hand family lineages, being Blackfoot and Navajo don't help either. He says this legend has been told in both tribes and has been passed down for many generations," Dad said and reached for a cookie. "He also said it was a skin walker that tore the bunkhouse apart the day you and Jace went to acquire that bear claw." He paused thoughtfully. "The fact that he believes that grizzly is a skin walker will spook the other wranglers."

"You wouldn't have any information to add to that, would you, Kerry?" Rob asked, sitting down at the counter.

"No. What would make you think I would know anything?" I struggled to keep my voice even.

13

"I just thought your friend Josh might have had some insights on the matter. He was asking about the dates of the kills, like it might mean something." Rob asked as he looked at me. Concern furrowed his brow. "I thought he might have passed that information onto you, that's all."

Josh Matheson and his sister Nakiya were the grandchildren of the Blackfoot's Shaman, Wolf Talker. I'd met Josh when he'd brought Nakiya back to the ranch. She was interested in knowing more about the cave I'd found a few days before she arrived. Jace, being a vet, had hit it off with Josh, as Josh was going to veterinary school, too. But more important, Josh had been my mentor through the ceremonies at the powwow.

"No. He didn't say anything about it. Maybe he's still working on it." I forced out each word. I'd never lied to my family before and it left a bitter taste in my mouth. I didn't want them to worry nor did I want them in any danger. But the less they knew, the safer they would be.

"You mind telling us why you were so bent on getting that bear claw from Ross Stevens' ranch hand?" Dad asked, sitting down beside Rob. "What's wrong with the bear claws in the barrel inside the barn that we collected

14

from the bear hunts over the years?" He reached for another cookie.

"Oh those. Well, I found out at the powwow that one of my spirit animals is the bear. I'd remembered that Ross Stevens' ranch hand had shot the claw off that grizzly and we went over to ask him if I could have it. I forgot all about those in the barn," I said, acting surprised, and closed the lid on the container of goodies I was taking with me. "I guess that claw was fresh on my mind what with all the talk and everything."

"When did you start believing in spirit animals and that stuff?" Steve mused. "Wouldn't have anything to do with a little Indian gal, would it?" he chuckled.

I could feel a flush of warmth starting at my chest and spreading up to the top of my head.

"Whatever," and rolled my eyes at them. However, that was one question I wasn't going to answer until this was over. My life had been simple before Shadow, my dog and I had found the cave over a month ago. That cave had put me on the path of a life and death quest.

"Do you have everything you're going to need?" Mom asked, putting two more crepes on my plate.

15

"Yes, Mom, I believe so. I went over my list of things to take again this morning. I have everything," I said, watching her. I could tell there was something else on her mind though, and wondered how long it would take before she let it out. I figured she'd wait until there were just the two of us in the kitchen. I was almost finished with my crepes when she sat down beside me at the counter.

"Kerry, I can't get rid of this feeling that you're in danger. Is there something you want to talk about or you need to tell me?" she asked, ruffling my hair.

"No, Mom. Why would you think that?"

"It's just that ever since you found that cave, I've seen a change in you, and this episode with that bear---- just promise me you'll be careful."

"I promise, Mom. What could possibly happen at the school?" I quizzed, and gave her a hug.

The screen door opened and Jace walked in carrying a pail of milk. "You about ready to get this show on the road, Kerry?" he asked, placing the pail in the sink. "You don't want to miss your train."

"I'm ready," I answered, gulping down the rest of my milk. I hurried to my room to get my suitcases, Shadow right behind me. I picked up my camera putting the strap around my neck. It wouldn't do to forget that since it was the reason I was going two weeks early to the school. I was getting a good reputation for my photography and that was why I had been invited to the school early; to take pictures of the animal life around the school to use in class. I had even kept my little secret: I could mind-speak with the animals to get their photos.

"Shadow, I wish you were going with me," I mind-spoke with him and wrapped my arms around his neck.

"I'll be on watch here, while you're gone. Your spirit bear will be watching over you, but at a distance. Crow, Raven, Fox and the White Wolf will contact you at the school to work on your shape shifting," Shadow mind-spoke in return. Picking up my luggage, I took one last look around my room. I thought how afraid I'd once been about mind-speaking with the animals whose pictures hung on my wall. Back then, I'd had to concentrate with my camera, eye to the viewfinder to mind-speak. Maybe someday we would cross paths and I could thank them again. The fear of mind-speech was gone and now it was as natural as talking out loud.

******

We pulled up to the train station with ten minutes to spare. I checked my baggage in, except for my camera bag, and then we sat down on a bench in front of the window. The view was to the north, and I thought it wouldn't be long before snow would cover those mountains.

"Try not to dream while you're away," Jace said, looking at me earnestly. "We and the other ranchers can't take any more losses."

I looked at him and scrambled for words. I'd never asked for the dreams. However, their impact on us and the others had been costly. I couldn't promise him I wouldn't dream, especially when my thoughts were on Nakiya. But knowing she was back in Tennessee, and in a couple of more weeks would be in Chicago going to the University, I felt somewhat more at ease.

"You know I have no control over them. However, learning how to control my shape shifting, and using my gift with my taxidermy, I'll be too tired to dream."

"Yeah, and when you shape shift, be extra careful who you're around. We don't want word getting back to the ranch that Mom and Dad have a shape shifter in the

18

family," he said with a serious look. "You call me if you need help with anything!"

We heard the train whistle and walked out onto the platform. I gave Jace and Shadow a hug, and then stepped onto the train car.

"I'll call you in a couple of days," I shouted and then I hurried to find a seat so I could wave goodbye.

As the train pulled out of the station, I felt emptiness in the pit of my stomach that loneliness was filling up. I would miss my family, but Shadow was a part of me, and now that I had mind-speech with him, I would miss him even more. We had a bond, a bond that went beyond friendship. I didn't know the distance we could mind-speak, but this would give us an opportunity to test it.

"*Shadow, can you hear me?*" I mind spoke, about a mile out of town.

"*Yes, Kerry, I can hear you,*" he replied.

"*That's great! I'll check in when I get to the school.*" I listened to the clink of the iron-wheels and felt the easy motion of the train as we rolled across the miles toward my destination. I was so tempted to close my eyes and sleep, but at the same time I was afraid that if I did, I would dream.

I settled on admiring the beauty of the country. From the town of Libby to almost Browning, Montana the pine-covered mountains were majestic. The different shades of green from the Ponderosa and lodge pole pines to the red, yellow, blue and purple wild flowers that covered the ground were all beautiful to my eyes. The sight could lure you into another world of the rugged west. The spirits that roamed this land, both white and Indian alike with their stories both courageous and heart-wrenching, made up the legends and myths of Montana.

I searched the tree line for Shawgun, wondering how far he would follow me. If he couldn't feel Moon Dancer's or my presence, would Shawgun play the waiting game? Would he wait until I went after my last gift? I was hoping he'd wait, because with figuring out how to control my shape shifting and learning taxidermy, my plate was full.

The anticipation of learning to channel my gift into my work was especially exciting. For years before I found the cave, I had dreamed about how life-like my animals would look with my skill as a taxidermist, never believing that one day I would have the gift to make that dream come true. Needless to say, when Moon Dancer and I found one of his stolen gifts, the acorn-size Orb on Icebis, I'd been doubly gifted. Keeping the blue Orb on your person, the power flowed through your body, giving part of the animal's soul back when doing taxidermy. I could make them look alive.

Unfortunately, in the scramble to escape from Cradle Top Mountain on the planet Icebis, where the demon Shawgun had hidden one of the gifts he'd stolen from Moon Dancer, I swallowed the Orb; which also gave me the power to shape-shift. My spirit animal, White Wolf had asked Raven to put a spell on me, to disable my shape-shifting until I learned how to control the changes.

The landscape had changed dramatically as the train passed through Browning, Cutbank and Shelby to Havre. The picturesque mountains diminished, and now the scenery was of rolling hills, prairie, wheat fields, alfalfa and cattle grazing.

It was late afternoon when the train pulled into Havre. As I stood on the step waiting for the train to come to a halt, I called to Shadow, but there was no reply.

CHAPTER TWO

Once I stepped off the train and stood on the platform, I looked around. According to John Monroe's letter, there would be someone to meet me. When no one seemed to take an interest in me...

"Kerry McDaniels?"

I turned around and recognized the face before me from the picture on the schools' brochure. The instructor was about my height with acorn brown hair that curled up from beneath his tan Stinson. Sea blue eyes sparkled with pleasure through black rim glasses and his beard and mustache were neatly groomed. I'd guess he was in his forties which surprised me, as I thought he would be a fair amount older.

"Yes sir, I'm Kerry McDaniels," I said reaching out my hand to him.

"John Monroe," he said, accepting my hand in a solid grip. "I've looked forward to meeting you, Kerry. I was pleased that you were able to come to the school early. Is this all your luggage?"

The steward had retrieved my two bags and set them down beside me. I thanked the steward and gave him two bits.

"Yes, the two bags Mr. Monroe are all I have. I'm excited to get started, sir."

"Just call me John, Kerry," he said and lifted one of my bags before walking down the platform. I grabbed the last one and hurried to reach his side. Going down three steps, I noticed a blue pickup parked next to the building. John continued toward it and put my bag in the back. I placed my other bag in the back, but kept my camera bag with me when I stepped up into the cab.

"Kerry, I know you planned to stay in town with the other students and ride the bus out to the school, but I have accommodations for three students at the school and wondered if you would mind staying there."

"That would be great, thank you."

"I was hoping you'd feel that way," he said, turning out of the parking lot onto the highway.

Looking around the scenery, I only noticed a few slight differences riding out of town than I did from the train coming in. Here, the rolling hills were slightly higher and the trees appeared to follow along the Milk River, then into the town of Havre.

I knew fifteen students were enrolled in the course. I felt a great relief knowing there were only two others that would stay at the school. My secret would be easier to keep hidden from two students rather than from fifteen.

As we drove the 30 miles to the school, I was getting a little worried about all the openness and how I was ever going to practice my gift with no seclusion.

"What stirred your interest in taxidermy, Kerry?" John asked, looking over at me.

"It's the only thing we don't do at the ranch as far as the outfitters part of it. I've always felt close to the animals. I prefer capturing their beauty on film than causing their death," I said, patting my camera case.

"I hope you brought pictures with you. I would enjoy seeing a few."

"How did you know I did photography?" I asked, shifting in my seat.

"One of my clients showed me photographs that you had taken. I was truly impressed. You seem to capture, mm . . . , Kerry I'm not sure how to explain it exactly, perhaps it's the essence of the animal. They seem to have a bit of magic to them. Maybe working with animals the way I do to preserve them is why I would see that in your photos."

"I was surprised when I received your letter and excited with your request," I said, rubbing my hand against my thigh. "Did you have anything in particular in mind?"

"Well, yes," he said, pointing to the tree line about a mile away. We'll start out with birds; you'll find that we have quite a variety. I was hoping you would be able to get a few pictures before school starts. It's easier for the students to work the forms if they have a picture to look at."

I was relieved when we reached the school building. Out behind the school about a half mile there were larger rolling hills, taller grasses and shrubs in the opposite direction of the area that John said the birds frequented.

As soon as we pulled into the school parking lot, I grabbed my bags out of the back of the truck and followed John into the building. We turned right and proceeded down to the very end of the hallway.

"I think you will like these rooms. Your room and mine are the only ones with private baths. I stay throughout the week during sessions. The other two will share a bathroom, and then of course there are public facilities outside the main class room," he said, opening the door to my room.

The room was fairly large. It held a bed, dresser, a desk and chair, and one overstuffed short couch covered by wildlife patterned material that looked like it had seen better days. Maybe it was sun faded from sitting next to the window.

"This is what I think you will really enjoy," he said, opening another door in my room.

"This is great!" I exclaimed, looking at the dark room. "It's easier and faster when the dark room is close while developing a lot of pictures."

"I thought you would enjoy the convenience having the dark room next to your room," he said, sounding pleased. "We just shifted some things around. I'll leave you to get unpacked and when you're done I'll show you around the school. Then we'll go get something to eat."

"Sounds great to me, I shouldn't be too long," I responded, then watched as he left my room shutting the door behind him. I set my bags on the bed, and laid my camera on the desk. I put away my clothes and placed my goodies on the desk as well. The window was large and I slid it open to look outside. I was delighted to see that the access through the opening would be adequate to climb in and out. Looking out my north window, this side of the building was about thirty feet from the east corner to the inner corner then turned and went north seventy feet making it an 'L' shape. I thought it strange no other widows were on this side other than mine? I closed the window and finished putting my things away. I picked up the envelope filled with pictures and went to find John. I saw him coming out of a room at the other end of the hall.

"You were right. It didn't take you long to put your things away," he said, as he waited for me to reach him, and then guided me toward large, double doors. "That door," John pointed to his left, "is the kitchen, small but efficient. This is it. This is where it all takes place," he said pushing through the doors.

I looked around in awe. "Are these capes the ones you are working on now?" I asked walking over sliding my hand along the hair on the hide. "It's so soft."

A hide was called a cape when it was ready to be worked over a form.

"You'll be learning how to do that. You know it really is how you take care of the animal's hide that gives it its beauty," he said, looking pleased at his work.

"Do you always start out with birds?" I asked, looking at the colorful pheasant that sit on his desk.

"Yes. Over the years it seemed easier for students to start out small, and with there being such a variety of birds that has worked best."

"Where do the students get their birds or animals for class?" I asked. I didn't like the thought of having to go out and shoot one for class.

"We have plenty of hunters around to take care of the shooting. I don't expect the students to make their own kills. Besides, I have the capes for this class in the freezer." He chuckled at my obvious sigh of relief. "I don't know about you, but I'm hungry and my wife should have supper just about ready." I followed him out to the truck and tried once more to mind-speak with Shadow, but again there was only silence. I wasn't sure how much further than a mile I could connect with Shadow.

John drove around to the back of the school and to my relief turned west on a well-traveled dirt road. John drove pass the area he wanted me to start taking pictures, then after another mile or so we arrived at the entrance of 'Shadow Valley Ranch'.

"You ranch besides teach at the school?" I asked.

The few barns and the white ranch style house I noticed were well kept. There was also a small bunk house and a bit further back, I saw three corrals. One housed a couple of horses, the other a few cattle. The third one was empty.

"Actually Kerry, I own the school, but I also love to teach. I do have a couple of other instructors who help me at the school from time to time. My wife and I both love to ranch and Rachael's half brother helps during the sessions I'm teaching. You'll meet him this evening."

"It's great to be able to work and play at what you love," I said, feeling the packet of pictures in the inside pocket of my jacket.

"Yes, it is. I could tell by the pictures you take, that you enjoy photography." He pulled around to the back of the house and his wife came out of the door to welcome us.

I was surprised when I saw her, realizing by her long black hair and copper skin that she was Native American.

"Rachael, this is Kerry Mc Daniels. Kerry, my wife Rachael," he said, putting his arm around her shoulders.

"Glad to meet you, Ma'am," I said, taking off my hat and reaching out my hand to her. She took my hand briefly, and she gave me a warm smile.

"Likewise, Kerry, I hope the two of you are hungry? Zeal said he would be late so we won't wait for him," she said, turning and leading the way back into the kitchen. The aroma reminded me of Mom's kitchen. I knew one thing for sure we were having hot bread. My mouth was already watering.

We sat down at the table which was set for four. Rachael set a large bowl of stew in the middle of the table, before she returned with the basket of hot bread. The stew had a variety of vegetables and thick pieces of venison which were smothered in a rich brown sauce.

"Kerry, when did your interest in photography begin?" John asked.

"I was twelve when I actually became serious with it. My sister does a lot of shows for the outfitter portion of the ranch, and they needed photos. I guess I had a natural talent for taking pictures, because I've been doing it ever since."

"Rachael, remember those photos I showed you? Kerry took those," he said, cutting another slice of bread from the loaf. Rachael's eyes brighten, and she gave me another warm smile.

"I brought others with me. They're in my jacket pocket," I said, looking at my jacket laying on the chair in the entry way.

I was enjoying my second bowl of stew, when Zeal entered the kitchen. I choked down the mouthful I had in my mouth, when I looked up startled to see the man standing across the table was Dark Antelope. It took us both by surprise. For a moment, I read hatred in Dark Antelope's eyes. His feelings hadn't change since the powwow prior weeks before. He'd been adamant about keeping me from participating in the sacred ceremony, and the relationship growing between Nakiya and myself.

"Zeal, this is Kerry McDaniels. He's attending school this session. Kerry, this is my brother-in-law Zeal."

"Howdy," I said, standing up and reaching my hand out to him. He took it and for a few seconds it felt like my hand was in a vise. I returned the pressure to keep my fingers intact. His message came across loud and clear; I could see in his eyes his feelings hadn't changed. He sat down at the other end of the table which I was thankful for, since I didn't want to have to look up at him every time I took a mouthful of stew. I half listened to them catch up on the day's events while my thoughts raced through my head. I didn't think I would have a problem separating myself from the other students at night to work on my uncontrollable gift. But now, with Dark Antelope, or Zeal, his white name, things would get complicated. This wasn't good and he was only a short distance from the school. I would be looking over my shoulder continually, at least until I made friends with the wildlife here. That would give me an advantage, unless he caught me in the middle of a transformation. Then I would be in trouble. Best not to think about it, I'd just have to be extra careful.

"Kerry, are you staying at the school or in town?" Zeal asked, his eyes hooded while taking in a spoonful of stew.

"I'll be...," I started to say and was interrupted by John.

"He'll be staying at the school. I asked him to come out early to do some photography for me before school started. Wait till you see some of his photo's, Zeal. I was really impressed."

Oh, no, I thought. I didn't need something else for Dark Antelope, or Zeal to be jealous of. Only hearing him speak in his Blackfoot language at the powwow I was taken by surprise to hear him speak English, and spoken exceptionally well at that.

"I'm sure I can show you some places that you can get some great wildlife shots," Zeal said, without smiling and continuing to eat.

"Kerry, are you finished?" Rachael asked. "I hope you left room for desert?"

"I am thank you. That was very good. But could I wait just a bit for desert?" I pleaded. My stomach was at its limit for the moment. "How about if I get those pictures and we look at them first. Then after, I'm sure I will have another hallow spot I can fill." Everyone laughed with that comment with the exception of Zeal. I could tell by their reaction to his soberness that it was not out of place here and I wonder if he ever smiled? At least, it did get me out of giving him an answer to his offer of being my guide. I retrieved the pictures from my coat and sat back down at the table.

I split the pictures in three groups and gave them each one, then sat back waiting for the questions.

"Kerry!" Rachael said with surprise in her voice. "I didn't know you knew Nakiya Masterson? Isn't that Nakiya, Zeal?" she asked, tossing the picture to him. Oh darn! I thought I'd taken out that picture of Nakiya with Maya and Shadow.

"Yes Sis, that's Nakiya," Zeal said, soberly.

"I met her when she and a group of girls came to the ranch for a rafting trip earlier this year."

"Let me see," John asked Zeal. Zeal hesitantly gave the picture to John and I gave an inner sigh of relief. I didn't think I would have gotten it back otherwise.

"That's my horse Maya and my dog Shadow. They took quite a liking to Nakiya." I said taking the picture from John.

We've known Nakiya from when she spent the summers with her grandfather learning the healing arts," Rachael said, looking at Zeal. "At one time Zeal and Nakiya had been promised by our grandparents, but many do not follow the old ways anymore."

"That will be our Nations down fall!" Zeal spouted angrily. We all looked at him. "Thanks Rachael for supper, but I must leave now." He walked out of the room and I heard the back door open and shut.

"I'm sorry about that. Zeal has a bitter heart since that promise will never be kept. I think he's been in love with Nakiya since the first summer that they met. But some things are not meant to be," she said reaching over and squeezing John's hand. "Are you ready for that desert now?"

We both nodded our heads yes and as Rachael went back to the kitchen John and I started going through the pictures again.

It was dark by the time we left and drove back to the school. John was still talking about some of the pictures I'd taken and was looking forward to me getting started capturing some of the birds that were around the area on film. We pulled up in front of the school and getting out we walked to the side door that was nearest my room.

"Kerry, you'll be staying at the school at night alone until the other students arrive. Then, I too will be spending most of my nights here. Will that be a problem?" He asked, unlocking the door.

"No. I'll be fine." I followed John inside and shut the door behind me.

"There's a pay phone you can use," he said walking to the other side of the hall and down about fifteen feet. "Do you have change on you?"

"Yes. I'll be fine. And thanks again for supper."

"You're welcome. Then I'll leave you and I'll see you in the morning. And thank you for agreeing to come early." With that, he left and I locked the door behind him and went into my room for some change. I called home and let Mom know that I'd arrived safe and everything was fine. I gave her the pay phone number in case she needed to get a hold of me. When I hung up the receiver, it echoed down the hall.

I went to my room, shut and locked the door. Taking the pictures out of my jacket, I found the one of Nakiya and placed it on the dresser. As I studied it, I couldn't help but wonder what she was doing, and if she missed me as much as I missed her.

I contemplated making a quick trip to the eastern hills and calling my spirit animals, but decided against it. Tomorrow would be soon enough. Besides not knowing where Zeal had gone, I didn't want to test my luck and run into him. I'd stay in tonight. I checked my window to make sure it was locked, before I put my equipment inside the dark room.

I took my boots off and laid my pants and shirt across the overstuffed chair and then snuggled down in the bed. I was alerted to the new sounds that emerged inside the building, sounds that could keep me awake tonight. I wondered if I would be blessed to hear the howl of a wolf in these rolling hills. Oh well, right now I'd focus on the crickets outside my window.

Chapter THREE

When I looked over at the clock on the wall, it read 9:10. Wow! I hadn't slept in this long since I was shot in the arm and who knew when before that. I reached down to pat Shadow and then realized I was alone and at the school. I was also relieved to know I hadn't dreamed.

I showered and dressed and heard the rumblings in my stomach. I hadn't thought about meals and how far town was from the school. Being without a truck made me think of the four days at the powwow I fasted. I didn't want to repeat that opportunity, at least I still had snacks left over that Mom had sent with me. I was opening the tin when I heard a knock on my door; closing the container again I shuffled to my door and unlocked it. Zeal (Dark Antelope) was standing in the hall with a basket in his hand. The scowl on his face proved he was one unhappy dude. I had a fleeting thought on whether or not he could look any meaner. Yeah, he could, as I watched the scowl deepen.

"Rachael sent this over earlier, but you were still asleep. She says you can heat it up in the kitchen," he said, handing me the basket.

"Thanks. And thank your sister for me," I said, taking the basket from him.

"John said if you want a ride to the bird area, I was to wait till you were ready."

"Zeal, I can manage. I'm sure you have things to do. Thank you for the offer, but I'll be fine." I saw no change in his eyes. He took a quick scan of my room and stopped for a couple of seconds when his eyes found the picture of Nakiya. He looked at me again, then turned and left. I closed the door and locked it. A few moments later, I heard the truck engine start and then the tires spin in the gravel, as Zeal released his anger on the truck. I waited to hear the sound of broken glass from the front windows of the school. Luckily, they survived.

My stomach growled again and I opened the basket. Inside were biscuits, scrambled eggs, ham, butter and jelly. It wasn't the first time I'd eaten cold food and I didn't want to take the time in the kitchen to heat it up. The biscuits were soft and I easily made ham-n-egg sandwiches. I placed the basket outside my door and then ravished the contents that had been inside.

With my camera around my neck, a backpack filled with film, candy and my first aid kit, I locked my door, and then the outer door to the school. Excitement built as I began my day's adventure. I found the trail leading to the grove of trees I could see in the far distance. The trail wasn't well trodden as the grass lay in one direction but still had agility to try and stand erect. It made me think that whoever went out this way returned another direction. I was anxious to see how many trails lead away from the grove.

A few clouds splattered across the sky, but didn't look threatening. A red tail hawk flew over head in the direction of the grove of trees. I was hoping he would stay there long enough for me to reach him. The closer I came I realized the grove of trees spread further than I thought. I recognized the taller trees as Popular, providing a good wind break up here. Intermingled was wild Crab-apple, blue spruce and fir pine trees, along with huckleberry bushes. Looking at the mix I'd say this large grove had been planted years ago. I looked up when I heard the red tail hawk cry out.

"Well good morning Mr. Red Tail Hawk," I mind-spoke to him. I watched him as he appeared to look around for the mysterious voice. "I'm down here, if you'll look." A moment later he flew down and perched himself on a limb that was a couple of feet above my head.

"Mind-speech being used by a human, this will be a story worth hearing," he mind-spoke back and shifted his head to the left, his gaze scrutinized me from head to toe. "The only ones I know that use mind-speech are Indian shamans and not many of them," the Red Tail Hawk commented. He gave me another once over before he spoke again. "I can see you're not an Indian." He hopped down to a branch that was just above my head.

"No. I'm not Indian, but part of my soul is."

"Indeed. This is getting more intriguing, your name mind-speaker?" He asked

"My name....."

"His name is Spirit Walker."

"Crow! It is so good to see you." Crow was my spirit animal that had led us to the top of Cradle Top Mountain where Moon Dancer and I had found the blue orb. "I wondered how long it would take you to find me."

"You have not been lost. Your spirit animals and I have always been near you. We were waiting for the right time to approach you. Good morning Hawk," Crow greeted the red tail hawk that sat on the limb just above my head.

I looked further up through the trees and saw Fox, Great Bear. Raven was riding on the back of White Wolf as they approached. It looked like a mist ascending but in the mist I could see them clearly. Maya and Shadow were not with them.

"No, Shadow and Maya are home keeping vigil," Great Bear said coming to a stop a few feet from me.

"You read my thoughts, Great Bear?"

"No, I read your face. You are searching for them."

"Hawk, I see the questions in your eyes," Crow commented, as he sat on my shoulder. "I will tell you Spirit Walker's story, while Raven works with Spirit Walker." Crow sat on my shoulder a few seconds longer before he flew up to sit near Hawk.

"Spirit Walker, when I lift the spell I'm not sure what will happen. Since you swallowed your gift and I've not heard of this being done before, you're treading on new ground here," Raven commented, sitting on a branch looking directly into my eyes.

"I understand." I swallowed hard forcing the extra saliva down over my Adams' apple. I put my camera down in a safe place so nothing would happen to it in case I started changing as soon as the spell was lifted. I first looked in all directions to make sure we were alone then walked back over and stood in front of Raven. "I'm ready." My hands were sweaty and my heart beat accelerated as I looked into Raven's eyes. I really didn't know what to expect. I felt myself being drawn into the dark depths of Raven's dark onyx eyes. My body tingled lightly as I listened to the words Raven chanted.

"In these two souls their gifts entwined,

The shape shifter sleeping on borrowed time,

I release the spell that holds him bound

This is the catalyst so your gifts may be found

Create your magic with the touch of your hand

44

An animal's essence their life to expand."

The tingling intensified until ocean waves were rolling through my veins. I staggered and reached out for a tree branch to steady myself. The pressure started to build at the top of my head. At any moment I thought it would explode. The world around faded to black and I wondered if I was going blind. And then–it quit. My body went still. The pressure eased and my breathing slowed. I sat down on a fallen log and looked up at Crow. I took my hat off and wiped the sweat from my brow. Crow and the others were watching me intently. My breathing returned to normal, as I stretched my body out, moving to make sure I didn't have any lumps anywhere that had gotten stuck from whatever it was that had rolled through my body.

"How are you feeling Spirit Walker?" Great Bear asked, taking a step closer to me.

"I feel fine. I...feel warm, I feel ...." I put my hand on my stomach that was starting to churn. "I feel like something is building. Oh! No! Here it comes, Moon Dancer!" I could feel my body changing. I thought of a rabbit at the last second, and found myself landing on four paws. Sprinting through the trees, I turned into an antelope, and then sprung up the ravine as a mountain lion, wolf and a buffalo. My arms spread out as I lifted off the ground. Turning around, I flew back to where we had started. After my feet touched the ground, I rolled and shifted back into myself.

"Why didn't you warn me?" I heard Moon Dancer's strained voice ask. I sat for a moment and fought to control my breathing as my lungs gasped for air. Once my lungs quieted, I waited, shell shocked from being turned inside out again.

"I'm sorry Moon Dancer. I didn't think we would shift as the spell was lifted," I sighed. "I yelled at you, but apparently not soon enough."

"I thought you wouldn't need me until we went after Shawgun, but I was wrong. You're definitely going to need help getting this shape-shifting under control," he mind-spoke solemnly.

White Wolf trotted over to us and sat down on his haunches. "I too am surprised that you started to shift after the spell was lifted. What were you thinking of at the time?"

"I was thinking of the escape from the mountain."

"You were caught up in your fear," Raven replied. "You are going to have to control your fear. That has been an issue for you, especially with things contributed by the spirit realm. But I'm thinking any strong emotion could start you to change, even anger."

"Sounds like I'm going to have to keep a rein on all my emotion until I get this under control."

"I can help, to a point," Moon Dancer admitted. "However most of the control is going to have to be you. I know we can sense each other's feelings, but controlling them is another thing."

"Spirit Walker, just out of curiosity," Raven asked, "why did you choose a rabbit to change into first?"

"Well, I thought if anyone was to see me as a rabbit I would be able to get away faster or hide easier than a larger animal."

"But you did change into a larger animal. A buffalo is harder to conceal especially in open prairie," Great Bear mused. "Have you thought about how you would explain shape-shifting to someone who might see you?"

"No. How could I explain this phenomenon? Who would understand?"

"You would have serious consequences," said Moon Dancer. "People act out of fear at things they cannot explain and the pale faces are the worst. No offense intended. But, this will cause you serious consequences," Moon Dancer spoke with grave concern."

"Okay, then what is the first thing I need to do, White Wolf?"

"You'll need to analyze your body, note any change in the way you feel inside or outside."

"What was the first thing you felt when you started to change?" Raven asked.

"*Someone comes,*" Crow mind-spoke. "*We will meet with you tomorrow.*"

"Hawk will you pose for me?" I asked as I reached for my camera. I was taking the second picture when Zeal came up the path carrying a twenty-two.

"I see you have found a Red Tail Hawk. He will look great stuffed." I saw him raise his gun to take the shot.

Jumping over the rotting log I threw myself into his side throwing him off balance.

"Why did you do that?" He yelled at me angrily shoving me back over the log.

"Walk lightly Spirit Walker," I heard Moon Dancer say calmly. "You don't want to shift in front of Zeal. That will only give us more problems." I took a deep breath trying to calm the churning in my stomach.

"Sorry Zeal I wasn't through taking pictures of him, and now you have scared him off."

"No? I'm sure one picture was enough and now we don't have a hawk for class," he growled.

"If you're going to kill my subjects, please do it when I'm not around." I hissed. "Is there some other reason that has brought you out here besides shooting the birds?"

"Rachael sent me to tell you supper is early tonight. They are leaving to go to Chinook and won't be back until later tomorrow morning. So if you're ready, we can leave." With that he turned on his heel and left in the same direction.

"It won't take much to set him off," White Wolf spoke. "I can feel the tension between the two of you. He harbors ill feelings for you for several reasons, and given the right circumstances your life will be in greater peril."

"What am I to do?" I asked, putting my camera in its case.

"Stay out of his way as much as you can Spirit Walker," offered Great Bear, "It may be easier for you to practice shifting at night. Red Hawk said he would spread the word you are a friend; and we'll ask the other wildlife to warn you of any intruders. He also said to thank you for saving his life."

"When I see Red Hawk, I will tell him he is welcome. I better go now. Tomorrow night I will meet you here." I put my case over my shoulder and followed the same path that Zeal had taken.

I could see Zeal's impatience as he sat in the truck tapping his fingers on the steering wheel watching me approach. I quickly stepped up into the truck and shut the door. He started the engine, made a U-turn and followed the road back out. We sat in silence on the ride back to the ranch. I didn't know what we could talk about without putting more tension between us, so I leaned my head back on the seat my hat covering my eyes.

******

I set Rachel's basket on the step and fished through my pocket for my key. I grabbed the handle again as the door swung open. Securing the lock, I moved on to my own door.

Lying on the floor in front of my door was the tiny piece of paper that I had jammed between the door and the casing. A trick I had learned to tell if someone had entered my room without my knowledge, had worked well before. I cautiously opened the door and flipped on the lights. It was empty. I locked the door behind me. After setting Rachel's basket on the desk, I surveyed the room. Only one thing appeared to be missing, Nakiya's picture was no longer on the night-stand. I checked around the furniture before realizing that it had been taken.

"Zeal, darn you," I rasped looking around for anything else that might be missing. Strange I knew that was all. "Darn you!" I felt the energy building in my belly as my anger grew.

"Spirit Walker calm down"

I pushed Moon Dancer back in my mind and concentrated on a mouse feeling the change start. I looked out two little beady eyes as I scurried around the room and then feeling my tail shorten, I change to a rabbit and then back to mouse. After several times shifting while my anger receded, I found myself laying on the floor once more, my sides heaving. Feeling like I'd run a 10K race or something, I rolled onto my back.

"That was a close call," stated Moon Dancer. "At least you were able to keep the animals small. I don't know how you would have explained any damage to the room."

"You're right there, Moon Dancer. I concentrated on the mouse and the rabbit until I felt my emotions calm.

"Well, maybe a lesson was learned this evening. If you're back to calm, I'll leave you now, but I suggest you have Raven bind your gift. If someone were to see you, it would be hard to explain."

I felt Moon Dancer's presence leave and pushed my body up off the floor. He was right; I needed to have Raven bind this gift until I had control. One arm stretched upward and then the other one. Feeling the blood flow return, I gently felt along my sides feeling for any abnormalities. Finding me all in one piece I checked the lock on the door and the window. More than likely Zeal had a master key. Keeping anything I valued out of sight until school started would be priority, not that I really had anything he'd be interested in other than Nakiya. Realizing I had only brought the one picture of her, I checked in my pocket for any change. Yes, I had enough to make two phone calls. My steps broke the silence in the hall and putting my dime in the pay phone I was surprised how it echoed.

"Hi Jace, how's things going on the ranch?"

"It's been quiet. How are things there?"

"Good. John has me staying at the school, did Mom tell you. I have a dark room off from my sleeping room. I..."out of my peripheral vision, I thought I saw something pass the exterior glass door, the nearest exit from my room.

"Kerry," I heard Jace say.

"I was just saying I've shifted twice without control other than the second time I did manage to keep the animals small."

I looked up and down the hall. I think I'm just spooked knowing Zeal had been in my room. Zeal wouldn't physically hurt me here at the school I was sure of that, but what if...My hand went to the bear claw around my neck. I put the phone back up to my ear.

"Have you talked to Josh?"

"Kerry I haven't talked to Josh since you left and things have settled down around here. But I'm not taking any chances with that Grizzly, you know who I mean. I talked Dad into keeping those new bulls corralled up at the Idaho spread. There haven't been any killings up that far."

"That's a good idea. Would you do me a favor and send me another picture of Nakiya. There should be some in the dark room with pictures of the powwow."

"Sure, where do you want me to send them?"

"Send them to Havre's post office, general delivery. I already spoke to them."

"I'll do it tomorrow."

"Thanks, Jace and give Mom a kiss for me and I'll call again this weekend." I hung up the phone and walked back to my room and locked the door behind me.

The window curtains were closed, but I checked the lock again and starred out into the darkness. Everything was still, not even a slight breeze disturbed the wild grass.

I stripped down to my boxers and laid my clothes across the overstuffed chair by the window, pulled the covers back and crawled into bed pulling the covers backup under my chin. My eyes closed. I felt myself rising from the bed.

"No. No, I can't dream, too much at stake."

"Spirit Walker." I heard my name called. I opened my eyes and in the distance I saw White Wolf, but it wasn't his voice I heard. This voice I didn't recognize. Gliding past me was an owl. The owl's wing span had to be close to five feet. White and light brown feathers with black wingtips s were black barred across both wings. Grey, white and light brown covered his chest. As he turned his face toward me an quarter inch black band surrounded his face and the large yellow eyes held mine.

"Spirit Walker, I'm Night Eagle," the Owl conveyed in my mind. *"I am one of your spirit animals."*

"Not to be rude, but I don't want to dream. I don't want my family hurt."

"Spirit Walker, relax. Shawgun will not feel your vibrations this night."

I felt my breath ease pass my lips, as I had been holding it. I should have been cold as the nights were cooling off in preparation for winter, but looking at my arms I had no goose bumps.

"Night Eagle, I didn't think I would meet another of my spirit animals until I hunted the demon, Shawgun. Are you here to help me with my shape-shifting?" We were closing the distance quickly to my spirit animals. I felt no movement from Moon Dancer in the back of my mind. I would let him sleep. "White Wolf, this is unexpected, however I'm happy to see you."

"Spirit Walker, Night Eagle, there is evil being cast this night," White Wolf said.

"Not Shawgun. I'm not ready to face him."

"No, Spirit Walker, this evil does not come from the demon Shawgun. Night Eagle will guide you to the source."

I seemed to be flying beside Night Eagle over open ground in the moonless night I saw nothing but a dark sea of prairie grass until we spied a campfire in a ravine, a lone person sat before it. We watched this person, a man it looked like, as we drew closer, his back still to us. He started to chant and out of several bags that lie in front of him, he removed a small amount of some kind of plant leaves and placed it in a bowl in his left hand. I startled when he picked up the rattle snake that was coiled next to him. Holding the head of the snake, he pressed the fangs down over the edge of the bowl, venom eased down the side. He tossed the snake to the side, and then picked up a small wooden spoon mixing the venom and herbs together. A cloud formed, but never went over the rim of the bowl. The chant was not one that I'd heard at the powwow, nor in Wolf Talker's teepee.

We hovered a moment, his face remained intent on his potion, so we slowly moved around him. His long ebony hair lay across his shoulders, his face painted half red, half black.

"Zeal/Dark Antelope."

"Yes, Spirit Walker. The mixture in the bowl is brewed for you," said Night Eagle. "His hate for you is as poisonous as the venom he milked from the rattle snake. Caution is in the wind; for you are in great danger. You..."

Dark Antelope jerked his head up.

I shot up out of bed, my heart pounding, my forehead beaded with sweat. I threw the covers back and got up and made it into the bathroom for a drink of water. Dream walking, I'd been dream walking with Night Eagle. The ranch and Shawgun, I needed to call the ranch. The clocked read 2:18 a.m... everyone would be asleep. What was it that Night Eagle had said, think, think. Ahhhh yes, he said Shawgun wouldn't feel this dream. Taking in a deep breath, I let it out slowly and shuffled back to the large overstuffed chair. Pushed aside my clothes and sank down into the cushions as my heart slowed, I finished my glass of water and pulled the window curtain back.

The moon started it's decent as it escaped the black clouds that had hidden its glow earlier, now was shining down on another enemy. Tomorrow night the moon wouldn't be as full when I would start to learn my skill to shape-shift. However, I would be exposed if someone was to follow me. I would be mindful that no one followed me. I would be an easy target for Zeal/Dark Antelope as I learned this skill.

Wide awake now, I decided to write Nakiya. I wondered if she knew I would be seeing Dark Antelope when I arrived at the school. Did she know of the conflict that loomed between the two of us, or that he was angry that she didn't follow the old tradition? I decided to mention that he helped here at the school and see if she would write back with added information about him.

When I finished, I asked her to send it to the post office general delivery. I didn't want Zeal to know we were corresponding.

My shoulders ached with tension and I rolled them feeling them ease. Sleep would help relax me, so I turned off the light and slid back inside my covers.

CHAPTER FOUR

I felt something against the door when I pushed it open. Another basket had been dropped off and I set it next to the wall taking out the banana and then shuffled to the pay phone. With the phone receiver in hand I placed my coin into the black box and listened to it clink to the bottom as I waited for the dial tone so I could call home.

"Rose Feather Outfitters," Mom spoke like a professional secretary.

"Hi, Mom. How are you and how are things on the ranch?"

"Kerry, hi sweetheart, I'm doing fine and it's busy. I'm fixing hobo dinners for your brothers to take out with them. They're going up early to find any strays before they start the roundup. How are you doing?"

"I couldn't be better, unless I was home. How's Shadow?"

"Good. Oh Kerry, I was going to call you later. Nakiya called. She told me her Grandfather is ill and she and Josh was flying up to spend some time with him. She mentioned that they think he might have pneumonia."

"When were they coming up?" I asked, running my fingers through my hair as I started to panic. As long as Nakiya was out of Montana I thought her safe from Shawgun. I also thought that at the powwow until I developed pictures and saw Shawgun in the background.

"Saturday," she said, "Their aunt is picking them up in Great Falls. Nakiya said she would call you Sunday morning."

"Okay. Love you Mom." When I hung up the receiver it echoed off the walls in the hall, but I was getting use to the sound. My mind replayed Mom's words as I ambled back to my room. I picked up the basket before I went back inside, and twisted the lock on the door automatically behind me. I set the basket on the desk, whatever was inside smelled good, although I'd lost my appetite. Josh would keep Nakiya safe, besides her grandfather was a powerful Shaman. Even ill he'd have safe guards to protect her, I was sure. I mindlessly started to peel my banana when I heard a knock on my door, laying it down on the basket I hurried to change out of my pajama bottoms into my Levis before I answered.

61

"Hi John," I was surprised and relieved to have him standing in the doorway.

"I wondered if you cared if I went with you today Kerry?"

"No, I wouldn't care at all. Come on in and I'll finish getting dressed. Oh, and thanks for the basket that was left.

"I guess Zeal must have put that together for you this morning. Rachael left in the early hours as she was going to Chinook to visit a friend and work on a quilt.

"Well, tell him thanks for me. I'll only be a minute." Walking back into the bathroom I closed the door. My stomach knotted, and beads of sweat broke out on my brow as I gripped the sink. I was glad I'd not eaten the banana thinking of it lying on the red and white checkered cloth on top of the basket. Maybe it was alright, perhaps it was the rest that was tainted, but I wasn't about to take the chance. This is one meal I would gladly go without. Running the cold water I let it flow through my fingers and then splashed it on my face. Thinking about Zeal mixing that concoction last night in my dream knotted my stomach again. Attending to my own food until school started sounded like a good idea.

******

"Kerry if you don't mind I have a couple of other places you can take pictures."

"Any place you want to go will be fine with me. If we're going toward town, I have a few things I need to pick-up, if that works for you."

"Sure we can stop on the way back and I have a soda in the cooler if you want one," John said stepping into the truck. I smiled and flipped the lid on the cooler open and grabbed a coke.

Before stopping at the reservoir we rode along the Milk River where there were plenty of trees that hosted numerous birds.

"I thought after you took some photographs we could go fishing for a while," John said as he pulled up beside the tall wind break trees. "I think it would be great if you could capture a few of the small animals that make their home here." He pointed to a pair of prairie dogs that crested the top of their burrow. I've asked that the hunters who supply the animals for the school to work away from our area."

I smiled in agreement. *"Hi, fellows. Care to pose for a picture?"* I mind spoke as they looked at us inquisitively.

"A human that can talk, how quaint," the biggest prairie dog returned.

"Your manners," the other one said and stopped grooming her companion's ear to add, *"You must be Spirit Walker. Red Tail Hawk has been spreading the word that you would be in this area for a while."*

"For awhile," I stated and then pretended to get the right angle as John sat up on the tailgate.

"We'd be delighted to pose for you," the smaller prairie dog replied.

The two were fun to capture doing little stunts but always faced the camera to expose their faces.

"Spirit Walker is here taking pictures!"

I heard the chatter in my mind coming from the nearby trees. I couldn't help but smile.

By early afternoon I'd gone through two thirty-six frame rolls of film, capturing most the birds and small creatures in the vicinity. John had stayed seated on the tailgate of the truck and was quiet the two hours I photographed. Putting my camera back inside its case, he finally spoke up.

"I would never have believed it if I'd not seen it with my own eyes," he said, looking at me speculatively.

"Believed what," I asked setting the camera bag on the floor of the truck.

"If I didn't know better I'd say you talked to animals."

I started to laugh, "What would make you think that?"

"You might not talk to them, but you certainly have a magic with them. I can hardly wait to see that film developed," he said reaching into the back of the pickup. He handed me a pole and then picked up another and a tackle box.

"Grab that tote would you, I made us some sandwiches."

I retrieved the tote and accompanied him down a thin trail to the water edge. Scanning the area I happily concluded this was an excellent place to fish. The water was emerald green, a large log had been positioned for a couple of people to sit and easily cast. I could see no debris, and although I preferred river fishing, this was an ideal place to relax.

"Kerry, have you and Zeal met before?" John asked putting bait on the hook.

"Yes, why do you ask?"

"I thought so. You can feel the tension between the two of you. The first time at the house I just shrugged it off, but Rachael has mentioned it also. Can I ask where you met?" He cast his line out over the water and reeled once to stop his line.

I baited my own and cast it out. Satisfied with my line I sat down beside him before I answered.

"I met Zeal at the powwow in Browning. Nakiya's brother introduced him as Dark Antelope, that's when I also had the pleasure to meet their great grandfather, Wolf Talker."

"Really, you've met the Blackfeet's great Shaman. Hmm. I can see why that would have Zeal disturbed. Few outsiders have interacted with Wolf Talker for several years."

"Wolf Talker allowed me to participate in the sun dance ceremony."

"That would explain it further, and the fact there's something between you and Nakiya?"

I felt a tug on my line and stood up to reel it in. Perfect timing, keeping busy, I could avoid explaining more regarding the powwow and my feelings for Nakiya. I pulled the large fish in and secured the net under him bringing the netted fish and my pole back to the log bench.

"Are we having fish tonight?" I asked disengaging the hook.

"Sounds good to me and I'm sure Rachael would be appreciative. Kerry, keep alert around Zeal. His state of mind I've wondered about for a while, but since the powwow he has me really worried. Rachael is also concerned"

"I'll be careful. I wouldn't what anything to upset your family."

"Zeal leaves day after tomorrow to go back up to Browning. Wolf Talker has taken ill."

My stomached knotted. I was afraid for Nakiya. There was nothing I could do until I talked to Josh and my spirit animals. The only thing positive was I would be able to practice shifting without looking over my shoulder for Zeal.

I put the fish on a cut willow and strung a short twig up through the fish's gill and laid it in the shade. Baiting my hook again I cast it out and sat back down.

"What will happen if Wolf Talker dies, as far as having a Shaman for the tribe?"

"It usually falls to someone in the Shaman's linage with whom he has worked. Things have changed so much over the years; I'm not sure what will happen. When I married Rachael her parents had passed on. Zeal is her only sibling. We've enjoyed the school and the ranch which I owned before we were married. She has leaned toward non-tradition ways, and that hasn't helped with the way Zeal feels about tradition."

After stopping at the store for the things I needed, I placed the perishables in a cooler and we started the drive back to John's ranch. Rachael was getting out of her jeep as we drove up the drive. She stood and leaned against her vehicle and waited as we pulled up next to her.

"Did you have any luck today up at the dam," she asked as we stepped out of the truck.

"I believe we can help with supper, sweetheart," John said grinning as he pulled the nice string of fish out of the back of the truck.

She smiled appreciative and then walked into the house with us following behind her.

"I fixed a salad before I left this morning. So as soon as those lovely fish are cooked we can eat.

Forty-five minutes later, we were sitting outside at the table beside the grill when Zeal walked around the house. If I didn't know better I'd say he was surprised to see me. The surprised look on his face quickly dissolved and he continued into the house. The three of us looked at each other, Rachael shrugged her shoulders. We quickly helped Rachael take dishes into the house and John and I cleaned up the grill putting the garbage away so not to attract any unwanted visitors.

The sun was going down when John drove me back to the school and helped me carry my things and the cooler into my room.

"John I can puts my things away.

"Are you sure? I can stay and help," he said with his hand on the door.

"No, I'll be fine. Will I see you tomorrow or am I on my own," I asked as I started to take a box of crackers out of the sack.

"It's Sunday tomorrow. Why don't you take the day off? Rachael and I will be in Havre most the day. I'll talk to you on Monday." he said closing the door.

*****

After putting away my purchases I had bought in town, I started the process in the dark room. My thoughts kept going back to what John had said about watching out for Zeal. The basket! I put the film down going back into my bedroom, shut the door to the darkroom and turned on the light. I opened the basket and took out the plate full of food and placed it on the dresser.

70

Opening the window I was in awe of the afterglow of the setting sun, colors of purple, pink and gold stretched across the western sky. I searched for the Red Tail Hawk but didn't see him.

"Can someone tell me if this food is poisoned," I mind spoke hoping one of the animals in the vicinity would hear me.

I left the window open and sat down in the overstuffed chair. I busied myself by checking my film supply and replacing what I'd used as I waited patiently for a reply. Giving up that I'd caught anyone's attention I went to close my window when I saw him trotting towards me. I waited as he come closer and then stopped a few feet from my window.

"You must be Spirit Walker," he said sitting back on his haunches.

"Yes I'm Spirit Walker and you are?" I asked the coyote.

"I'm Jackal. How may I assist you Spirit Walker?"

"Jackal, can you tell if this food has been poisoned without endangering yourself?"

"It's known the coyote will eat anything and with that has come knowledge of good and bad. What is it that you wish to know about?" He asked stepping closer to the window.

I set the plate down outside on the ground and watched as he smelled the contents. It took him less than a minute before he looked back up at me.

"I would not advise that you eat this as it has been laced with something I can't positively identify. However it would make you very ill."

"Thank you, Jackal."

"You're welcome Spirit Walker." Jackal trotted back the way he had come and I disposed of the food that Zeal had left for me that morning. I was glad John and I had stopped at the store on the way back from our photo/fishing trip. I had all the food I would need until class started in five days. John, the other two students and I would be cooking our breakfast and supper. John had mentioned there was a cook that would come in and prepare lunch for all the students.

Last night I'd dreamed walked leaving my body and traveled with Night Eagle. That short voyage saved me from sickness or maybe even death. My spirit animals had saved my backside on more than one occasion.

*****

Seeing the radiating glow that came from the grove of trees I knew my spirit animals waited for me. I also knew I was the only one who would be able to see them.

"*We thought you'd never get here,*" Fox mind spoke, shaking his head as he looked at me and then over at White Wolf.

"Sorry. Guess I got carried away in the dark room."

"*Let's get started,*" said White Wolf, "*you might want to wake Moon Dancer. I've realized you will need his help until you can control the changes.*"

"This may take a few minutes," I said sitting crossed-leg on the ground. I closed my eyes and called to Moon Dancer. "Moon Dancer wake up. I need your help. We're going to try shifting, will you wake up?"

"*Yes, Spirit Walker, and thanks for waking me. Being tumbled around is frustrating and it's hard to focus. At least when I'm awake I can help you control some aspects of the changes. "*

"*Are you ready?*" Crow asked balanced on a low tree limb. "*You need to think of one animal, one small animal as Raven releases the binding.*

I thought of a prairie dog as I listened to Raven chant.

"*In these souls gifts are twined*

Sleeping, resting on borrowed time.

I release the spell that holds you bound

Shape-shifting mindfully is paramount."

I felt the tingling as before start at my toes and move up. Fisting my hands several times I focused on the prairie dogs and stood up. The tingling continued up my body and after it reached the top of my head I felt nothing unusual.

"What's happening, Moon Dancer? Why aren't we changing?" I took a deep breath and opened my eyes. My spirit animals watched me intently.

"*What are you feeling?*" asked Crow.

"I felt the tingling and then nothing."

"I believe Spirit Walker's shifting is determined by his feelings at this point," Moon Dancer spoke to all of them. *"Each time he has shifted it has been fear or anger that has released the change."*

Crow paced back in forth in front of us. *"This is unexpected."*

"Not really," White Wolf said. *"If you think about it, this gift was to enable Spirit Walker to give part of an animal's soul back into the animal's model as he worked his taxidermy. But when he swallowed it the magic of the Orb was infused with Spirit Walker's strong emotions. As in us when we fear we have an adrenaline surge for fight or flight."*

"So you're saying that the only time Spirit Walker can or will shift, is when he's angry or afraid?" Great Bear asked scratching behind his ear.

"I think so at this point. Tonight Spirit Walker was calm in mind and body having been working in his dark room." Moon Dancer commented.

"*This is an unexpected development*," Night Eagle said.

"*I can't follow him around all the time binding and unbinding this spell*," Raven expressed

"*This does cause more of a problem than we anticipated*," Crow surmised. Crow continued to look at me with intense black eyes.

"*The only thing I see going for you Spirit Walker*," said Moon Dancer, "is *that your personality is not prone to either one of those emotion. Well maybe the fear part but not to the extent of shifting. The thing I've noticed is when you're afraid in the first stage, you hold your breath before you go into flight or fight mode.*"

"Thanks, Moon Dancer. You've made me more aware of that, not realizing I had that habit. I guess that does make me feel better, but it doesn't take care of the problem."

"Crow I do have a question," I said, "If I was to get hurt, would I be able to shift?"

"*That could be debated, Spirit Walker. Say you were hurt as an animal, yet out of reach from another attack, I believe you would shift back to your human form, so you could take care of your injury. On the other hand if you were hurt in your human form, I don't believe you could shift as your body would hold on to its true form to heal."* Crow continued to pace and then stopped in front of me. *"There are so many variables and this is a rare phenomenon, we'll just have to watch and see. That means you will have to write notes after each episode so we can pinpoint certain characteristics and find a pattern."*

Great, one more thing to worry about, I thought.

"I need to mention that Spirit Walker is in great danger here," Night Eagle said.

"You think the demon Shawgun will come here for him?" Great Bear asked.

"It's not Shawgun," Night Eagle responded. *"He's in great danger by the hand of the warrior Dark Antelope. He has already made an attempt on Spirit Walker's life."*

"We had not foreseen this," said White Wolf. *"Are you sure it is Dark Antelope?"*

"*Yes. I took Spirit Walker with me on a night walk and if we had not spotted Dark Antelope, I fear Spirit Walker would be very ill, if not dying.*"

"*Spirit Walker!*" voiced Moon Dancer, "*You did not tell me of this.*"

"You were in your favorite corner of my mind asleep. I didn't think it important to wake you, since I was with Night Eagle and had seen the danger. In fact I made a new friend, a coyote named, Jackal, who told me the food that Zeal/Dark Antelope brought for me to eat was in fact poisoned. I have now gone to the store and have enough food to last until school starts. So unless he tries to do away with me in another way, I should be safe enough."

"*I think my sleeping time has been shortened. We can't lose to another adversary. There is too much at stake here.*"

"*I think that a wise decision, Moon Dancer,*" White Wolf remarked.

"Okay. Let me concentrate and see if I can get angry enough to shape-shift while you're all here."

CHAPTER FIVE

I thought of only one person that would make me angry enough to shift and that was Zeal/Dark Antelope. And the reason was not for trying to kill me but for taking Nakiya's picture off my dresser. I felt the heat inside rise up with the tingling coming up from my toes once more. The tingling was growing, not just a wisp from my toes but a torrent as I thought of him staring at her picture, of him placing his hand on her shoulder...It happened so quick I'd not thought of the prairie dog but as a...

My body contorted, feeling the bones pop, my muscles contract and lengthened. The next thing I knew I was looking through of a pair of golden eyes at my surroundings, my claws dug into the dry earth before I sprung up the ravine.

"Think small,"

I heard Moon Dancer whisper. I tried to down size my anger and shifted into a lynx. My thoughts strayed back to Nakiya and my body lurched back to the mountain lion.

"Concentrate, let the anger go now."

I heard myself scream at the rabbit that bolted out in front of me. Think small, I thought as I could almost feel the rapid thumping of the rabbit's heart. I shifted again into the lynx and turned back down the ravine, shifting again into a large calico cat before I shifted into my human form stumbling to my knees only a few feet from my spirit guides. I put my hands out in front of me to protect my face and felt the ground scrap across my palms. Rolling onto my side wheezing for air hoping my recovery would be quicker this time.

"*Much better, Spirit Walker,*" Crow said hopping toward me. "*I could see when you changed your thoughts. There will come a time when you can hold more than one thought at a time with clarity.*

Having Moon Dancer talk to me made the difference, or I'd been to the next county by now.

"*I think that is enough for tonight,*" Crow advised. "*However, we will try tomorrow night. The less you have to avoid others in the building the better. We have four more nights before the other students arrive, is that correct Spirit Walker?*"

"Yes, Crow." I nodded goodnight to the others and found the path back to the school. Looking overhead I saw that Night Eagle had followed us.

"I'm not worried that Zeal/Dark Antelope would show up tonight. In fact he left for Browning this morning. Wolf Talker is ill, Moon Dancer. John told me that Josh and Nakiya have both been called to Browning."

"I have seen Wolf Talker's spirit slip in and out between worlds. I believe he will go on to Icebis and not be reborn to this world again."

"Why would you think that," I asked puzzled.

"The freedom to roam Mother Earth is gone as is the buffalo. Small herds raised and regulated, and he does not like to see our people give up our traditions," he sighed.

"Will Nakiya and Josh be safe from Shawgun?"

"It's hard to see without our last gift, Spirit Walker. I do know many elders will come when the new Shaman is named. I feel Shawgun will not bother them at this time. He cannot harm Wolf Talker as he passes between worlds,

as you have Shawgun's claw around your neck binding him here.'

"So you think Josh will be named the new Shaman?"

"Josh is the eldest, but both he and Nakiya have been schooled in the old tradition and the skills that they would need to be the next Shaman."

"Will Nakiya be safe from Dark Antelope, Moon Dancer? I worry about her even if there will be many of your people there."

"You love her, Spirit Walker. I can feel your heart is full. You both walk a different path and will it merge, I do not know. But I feel she will be safe enough."

Unlocking the school door, I turned and waved goodnight to Night Eagle before I entered the school. I felt at ease becoming accustomed to the noises the building made at night. Moon Dancer had slipped back into slumber and I decided to finish cleaning up the dark room.

I smiled when I glanced at the pictures I'd taken that day. They were dry now and I took them down and put them into groups. I felt a twinge in my chest knowing that

John would have someone hunt and kill some of the animals I'd taken pictures of for class. The students needed capes, however it didn't ease my mind knowing the animals would be shot.

I finished up the last pile when I heard the phone ringing. Barreling out of my room I raced to the phone.

"Hello" I gasped, surprised I was winded, but I knew the reason had to be I was excited to get a call.

"Kerry hi, this is Nakiya."

"Nakiya, it's so good to hear your voice. Sorry to hear about your grandfather. How is he?"

"He has pneumonia. And he refuses to go to the doctor, here in Browning."

"I heard you were going up there. I didn't know you were there already. Did you get my letter? Is Josh with you? Do you think Josh can talk him into going to the doctor?" I rambled on excited that she had called.

"It arrived today and Josh will be up in a couple of days. He and Dad had a few things that needed finished before they fly up. Mother is with me."

"Well I'm glad you're not alone."

"Kerry I've been coming up here by myself since I was ten to learn from my grandfather. Why would you be worried if I was alone now?"

I rubbed the top of my boot up and down my calf. I didn't want to tell her about Dark Antelope she had enough to worry about with her grandfather's illness. And besides Dark Antelope I was worried about Shawgun. I wasn't there to protect her and I didn't know how serious Nakiya took the threat that was cast on her. Knowing she didn't have a hint that Dark Antelope could be a dark horse.

"It's just I don't know where Shawgun is hold up and..."

"Shawgun, who are you talking about?"

Crap. Josh knew about Shawgun and his intention. We had deliberately not told Nakiya, with her going to college in Chicago, we both thought she'd be safe there.

"Nothing, are you staying at your Grandfather's?"

"Mother and I both are. Between the teepee and the cabin we'll be fine. I wanted you to know Grandfather asked about you and if you still wore the bear claw."

"Tell him yes, and that I've met another of my spirit animals, Night Eagle."

"The owl. I should have known he might be one of your spirit animals by the way you walk with spirits. I will tell him. I need to get back."

"Nakiya, will you have Josh call me. I'm in my room usually after 6 pm. I've missed you." I couldn't stop myself from saying it and wasn't sure what she'd think about that. I was surprised when she answered me back.

"I've missed you to, Kerry. I'll have Josh call you. Good night.

"Goodnight, Nakiya."

*****

John picked me up Monday morning.

"Kerry I have another area to show you," he said as we drove out of the parking lot. "We'll probably see bigger game today, if nothing has spooked them. There's a little valley just east of here that's secluded. Someone from town said they saw a moose and her twins out there a couple of days ago. I'm hoping she's still there."

"That would be great. I have a great zoom on this camera."

"I told you that Zeal left for Browning. He told Rachael he wouldn't be back until the Shaman's health turned around or..."

"Nakiya told me he has pneumonia? I'm glad I was allowed time with him. Wolf Talker told me our paths would not cross again in this life," I said reaching for the bear claw around my neck."

"You were given a rare privilege that is for sure, Kerry."

We rode in silence the next few miles. I was feeling apprehensive that Moon Dancer might leave me for a short while if the Shaman was that ill.

"*No Spirit Walker, I will not leave you until our task is finished. We have much to accomplish before you return home for Christmas.*"

The turmoil in my stomach relaxed knowing I wouldn't be without Moon Dancer. I needed him to shape-shift. At least now I didn't have to worry about Dark Antelope showing up while I trained. Working on my emotions to create the shift, I could focus a hundred percent.

"We have one of the students coming in on Thursday. Harley, a cousin of Josh and Nakiya and on Sunday Roger Hopkins should arrive from Utah.

We stopped at the top of the knoll looking down into the large grassy valley.

"This is surprising." Trees were scattered throughout, unusual from the rest of the country where the trees were scarce.

"Yes. It's a well hidden secret. Actually we're on private property and I know the owner who gave me permission to bring you up here. He has your same views on animals," John said as he slowly drove forward, "he would like to meet you before you leave to go back to Libby. He was as excited about your photography as I was."

"Stop, over to your left," I said getting my camera out. John turned down into a small grove of trees and stopped. "I want to try and get closer but you can watch from here without being in danger. Moose are dangerous on their own but a mother and her young can be deadly as you well know."

"Are you sure Kerry you want to get closer? You can't take pictures of them from here with your zoom?"

"I'll be fine. I won't get any closer than I have to," I said stepping out of the truck.

I started down the hill, my camera around my neck. I sought out the moose with my mind. I saw her head come up and look around. She spotted me moving closer and pawed the ground tearing up the grass beneath her hoof, charged and stopped. "Easy girl, I just want to take your picture." She called to her young as they played away from her protection. She sprinted toward them, stopped and looked back at me as I spoke to her again.

She realized then, I was the one speaking to her, but I also noticed that Red Tail Hawk flew low over head which seemed to smooth her aggressive stance.

"*Ah, Spirit Walker, welcome to our valley,*" she said, and then nosed one of her calves around from her other side to stand next to its twin. The twins butted heads, then one calf slid coming to rest on its rear. I'd been taking pictures for a while when I heard the truck horn.

"Kerry, behind you; behind you!" John yelled.

Tuning around, I saw a skunk that was waddling towards me.

"*Good morning Spirit Walker. I'm Gilda. I'd like my picture taken too.*"

"Good morning Gilda. I'd be happy to take your picture," I mind spoke back to her as I glanced back up at John who was pacing back and forth. I waved to let him know I had seen the skunk and continued taking my snapshots.

My stomach growled and knew it was well after lunch. By the time I was through I'd captured deer, elk, a badger, Gilda a skunk, besides the moose and her twins. We defiantly had a variety of animals on film for the coming session. I was excited to get back to the darkroom to develop them.

*****

It was dusk when I left for the small ravine where we'd been practicing my shape-shifting. I was relaxed knowing Zeal had left for Browning and I didn't have to worry about him stumbling upon me or seeking me out. I smiled as I saw the glow at the mouth of the ravine. My spirit animals, what would I've done without them as they had been such an influence in the short time I've known them.

"You are right Spirit Walker to hold them in high esteem. Even after this crises is over your spirit animals will always be there to guide you,"

"Moon Dancer I see you are awake. Did you always follow your spirit animals?"

"Each animal has imprinted a part of himself on your mind and soul. It is up to you to listen. I've always listened to my spirit animals and to Mother Earth and stayed close to the Great One. They will never miss-lead you Spirit Walker."

Night Eagle called from overhead and descended, coming to perch on the shoulder of Great Bear.

"*I see you walk in a care free manner this night,*" spoke Great Bear.

"Yes, I'm more relaxed since I was told that Zeal has left for Browning. That knowledge will allow me to put my full concentration on controlling my shape-shifting."

"*I believe not all your attention is here. You fear for Nakiya, not that it's not warranted, but ease your mind as Josh/Running Wolf, will protect her and even as Wolf Talker is on his death bed, he is still very powerful,*" spoke White Wolf, "*now down to the matter at hand.*"

"*Tonight we will work on forming the animal in your mind and shifting without the use of your emotions,*" Crow said. "*Kerry I want you to think of an animal in your mind. Close your eyes. Do you have an animal?*"

"Yes," I replied thinking of a wolf. Wolves seem to hold a strong link with me since I'd saved the wolf at home from one of Anderson's traps and as White Wolf was the first to appear to me in my dreams.

"Good. Now study your chosen animal. Know him in great detail until he fills your mind. Until that is all you see. Study him as your hands scan over his entire body," Crow continued. His voice was soothing, smooth as velvet as he directed me on this new path. *"Go slowly looking for every detail, the shape of his body, the color of his eyes. Feel his strength flow through his form, his steady heartbeat. When he fills your mind completely give yourself up, blending your body with his. Keep his image in your mind."*

My hands followed the black and silver design of the wolf's coat as my fingers examined him from the tip of his nose to the large paws. I felt the steel hard texture of his nails as I explored leg and paw, the powerful muscles beneath his beautiful pelt to the black tip of his tail. Coming back around to face him, I saw the intelligence in his eyes as they studied me. I felt like I was in a trance and I was falling into the depths of his eyes, we started to merge. My arms were covered in fur and I felt my face start to elongate. My heart pounded, startled at the pain with this slow conversion, I panicked.

"Relax, Spirit Walker. You're holding your breath and shifting is painful if you stay ridged," whispered Moon

Dancer. *You're letting go of the wolf's image. Hold it in your mind until you see or feel nothing else. Feel the wolf's heart pump the blood through his veins, feel his breath move in and out of his lungs. Match your breathing to the wolf.*

"I can't, the bones in my face are breaking, I can't stand the pain," I cried out. I let go the wolf's image and fell backward landing on my back and the pain disappeared at once. "Ouch," I winched pulling a broken branch out from underneath me.

"*You have to overcome that habit of holding your breath,*" Great Bear remarked., "*it cuts off the oxygen to your brain, slows your reflexes making you an easy target for your enemy as it steals your energy.*"

White Wolf walked up to me and sat down on his haunches. "*Spirit Walker, pick up that rock beside you and tell me what you feel.*"

I picked up the hand size rock and turned my hand over and looked at the cold hard grey speckled object.

"It's cold and hard," I said looking back up at White Wolf.

"*All right,*" White Wolf said. "*Now close your eyes and concentrate on the energy that is flowing around the rock.*"

"Strange, the rock feels warm and I sense waves of movement around it."

"Keep your eyes closed."

I felt grains of soil replace the rock in my hand feeling the energy glide around my fingers, next blades of grass feeling the same energy.

"Yes I can feel the energy flowing from all of them."

"*Now I want you to feel the energy flowing all around you. Everything has its own energy that flows around and through us, just as our energy field flows with Mother Earth and everything in this universe. You felt the flow on Icebis,*" White Wolf continued. "*You can draw that energy to you when you shift. You just have to think of it surrounding you. Now let's try again and this time let yourself go.*"

"Moon Dancer, nudge me if I start to hold my breath."

"*I believe if you bring the wolf fully into your mind and feel the energy flow through you, you will shift easily.*

Lose yourself in the wolf, being only a shadow as I am in your mind."

I sat back on my heels, filled my mind with the wolf, his scent, the feel of his black and silver coat. As we merged I felt my face elongate and bone and muscle contort. The energy crackled around us until I looked out golden eyes at my spirit animals. I stepped forward on one paw, the others followed. Then I broke into an easy lope up the ridge. The wind blew gently against my fur and I raised my nose into the breeze picking up the scents around me. The hair along my back stood up catching the scent, evil.

A grizzly bear tore through the berry bushes coming right at me. I sank deeper into the wolf giving him free rein and felt our teeth exposed to the night air; a deep growl emerged from our throat.

The wolf lunged at the bear as the clawed arm come down missing the wolf's shoulder by fractions. Going for the throat the wolf was almost as tall as the grizzly as its jaw clamped down sinking teeth through the heavy pelt. The bear roared clawed down the side of the wolf raking fur and flesh.

"*Leap away,*" Moon Dancer yelled, feeling the flesh being torn from the wolf's side. With blurring speed the wolf leaped free blood running from its jaws and down its side. The bear roared and turned, disappearing back through the berry bushes, leaving behind blood stained leaves in its wake.

"Was that Zeal or the demon," I cried as the wolf staggered back down the ravine. Dizzy from loss of blood we fell to the ground. My spirit animals closed in around me as my strength ebbed.

"*Spirit Walker,*" Crow summoned,

I heard my name being called. It sounded so far but I just wanted to drift away. I wanted to distance myself from the pain.

"*Spirit Walker, you need to shift back into our human form. Come on Spirit Walker. How are you going to save Nakiya if you stay here and sleep?*" scolded Moon Dancer.

"Nakiya." I held her image in my mind. Shifting not thinking of the pain I would feel in my human form, I felt the wolf relinquish. My side and belly were on fire as I looked down at the claw rakes. How was I going to stop the bleeding?

"*Hang on, Spirit Walker. Help is coming*" I heard White Wolf say as I tried to keep my eyes open knowing if I let them close I would black out.

"Who's coming," I cried reaching for my backpack and the first aid kit I always carried with me.

"*Running Wolf approaches*" Crow said landing off to my right.

"Running Wolf, how can that be?" I asked as the pain swept over me. I tried to slow my breathing as my fingertips touched my backpack but I blacked out.

CHAPTER SIX

My eyes snapped open like blinds on a timer when I felt the cold substance hit my skin and then burn.

"Ouch, dang, Running Wolf, what are you doing here and what did you pour on me?" I rasped, and closed my eyes again.

"I'll answer your first question. I decided to drive my truck up so I had wheels and thought I would stop to see how you were doing? Good thing or you'd have probably died up in that ravine and the answer to your second question, whisky. Now hold still why I sew these rake marks up. These two are long and deep. You'll have scars from these."

"Thanks," I gritted and bit down on the leather strip Running Wolf put in my hand. The hook needle pierced through my skin and into the other side pulling the thread through and my skin together. The second stitch I bit down harder and felt a trickle of blood run down my back. Turning toward the window I avoided looking at my lacerations and knew exactly why I never wanted to be a vet or a doctor. I tried not to cry out and I couldn't keep the tears from running down my cheeks or the contents of my stomach from creeping up my throat. When I opened my eyes, the waste basket was beside the bed and I inched my head just over the edge.

"Oh crap," were the only words I got out before I started filling the garbage can. Josh's hand held my shoulder back and tried to keep me as still as he could.

I'd gone most my life without getting scarred up which was surprising living on the ranch, and in little over a month I now had two scars on my chest from the powwow, one on my arm from the gunshot wound Anderson gave me and now two claw rakes that ran down my side. I knew I couldn't keep them from my parents forever, but I had to until Shawgun was dead and my family was out of harm's way.

"Thanks," I said taking the cloth Josh offered me to wipe my mouth.

"Was this the demon, Shawgun?" Running Wolf/Josh asked.

"I don't think so. He wasn't able to touch me before when I held the claw, but I hadn't shape-shifted. However, I was in a wolf form and I still had the claw around my neck. No, I think this was Zeal/Dark Antelope. I thought he'd gone to Browning and I let my guard down."

"You know Kerry," he said as he continued to sew me up, "Shawgun could use him. The claw would have no effect on Zeal, Josh stated. "I know Zeal has reason to hate you, but he has always done things that were best for the tribe. I don't think he would do anything intentional to jeopardize his place on the council."

"Well, whoever it was has a chunk out of their neck. My wolf sunk his teeth in deep. I still have a copper taste in my mouth even after throwing up." I gritted my teeth again feeling the needle pass through my flesh.

"You'd still be hanging on to that bear if I hadn't told you to let go," said Moon Dancer.

"You're probably right," I mused.

"How is he doing?" I heard Red Tail Hawk ask as he landed on the window sill.

"Spirit Walker has lost a considerable amount of blood; he's weak but he'll be fine."

"I'll go tell the others. Thank you Running Wolf for your help," Red Tail Hawk said and then spread his beautiful wings and flew back toward the ravine.

"Yes, tell my grandson thank you. His timing couldn't have been better. I almost gave up hope of ever seeing my other lost gift.

"Moon Dancer and Red Tail Hawk told me to tell you thank you. I guess sometimes Moon Dancer hasn't much faith in me. But then I don't have much faith in myself in the mixture of things," I said feeling a small crescent form on my lips. "What am I going to tell John, when I see him?" I asked gasping.

"I think you will find that John knows more than what he lets on. Rebecca keeps in touch with what is going on within the tribe and you're participating in the Powwow wasn't a small thing. I doubt he knows about Shawgun, however, he knows how spirits can be controlled by others. The less he knows the better and the less danger you put Rebecca and him in. So unless he asked you straight out, I'd just tell him you're under the weather and that will give you a couple of days until you can get up and around."

"How long can you stay? I asked as I tried to keep my breathing even to lessen the pain.

"I have to leave in the morning, Kerry. I'm not sure how much longer Great Grandfather will hang on, and I need to be there before he passes into the spirit world. If whoever attacked you is hurt as bad as you say I doubt they will be back anytime soon. I'll check on Zeal when I get to Browning. Tell Moon Dancer he is welcome. I want him to find his other gift and will do anything to help."

"He heard you Josh and thanks you. I'm not going to tell my family. I know Jace would be up here if I really needed him, but with him being the only vet in the county, he's needed there."

"It looks like you're getting your shape-shifting down if you were able to fight off that bear," Josh said cleaning up the blood soaked rags and the items he used to sew me up with.

The two smaller lacerations he taped together, and after he smeared his herb concoction on the ones he sewed up.

"I don't know about that. We've been working on a new method, so I guess you can say I had a good start until that bear came out of the berry bushes."

"You survived which means Moon Dancer also survived. I'm going to fix you an herbal mixture to drink that will help build your blood back up. And before you ask, yes it will taste horrible, but you need to drink all of it. You're too close to needing a transfusion and I don't have the equipment with me to give you one."

"*It will help you Spirit Walker, hold your nose if you have to*," spouted Moon Dancer.

"Tell Moon Dancer that I added a small amount of skullcap," Running Wolf/Josh stated.

"*Tell him thank you,*" Moon Dancer said.

"And what does this skullcap do?" I asked, as I had acknowledged Moon Dancer seemed pleased.

"It will help you rest," Running Wolf/Josh said smiling.

He didn't say anything else but I felt there was a small conspiracy going on between him and Moon Dancer. He bandaged my battle wounds, and I lay back down, my eyelids encouraging me with their heaviness to sleep.

"When you wake Kerry, I'll be gone. Your wounds should be okay, but check them for drainage in the morning. I would suggest you stay down for another day. You shouldn't do any shape-shifting until those are healed as you would tear them open."

"Will you call and let me know how Wolf Talker is fairing," I asked. My words slurred.

"Yes. I'll call Friday night, sooner if...rest Kerry."

I turned onto my other side and groaned. I felt like I'd been breaking broncos for a week.

"Moon Dancer, how long have we've been asleep?" I asked as I pushed myself up to sit. *"Whatever Josh gave us, knocked us out."*

"Yes. You needed to sleep to let the herbs do their job healing." Moon Dancer remarked.

I stood up and staggered into the bathroom and looked at my watch that was setting on the sink. It was early afternoon and I was thinking it was Wednesday. Five more days and school would start. And I knew the other two boys staying at the school would be coming in this weekend.

There were also six tablets by my watch and a note that said 'take one every six hours'. The note under the small gauze pouch read, steep ten minutes and drink all of it. The words **all of it**, was underlined. I heard a knock on my door.

"Just a minute," I said, as I looked for a shirt to put on. Once that was done I wobbled to the door and opened it. A tall lanky boy with raven hair down to his waist, black eyes and a smile that showed a row of white teeth looked back at me.

"Kerry?"

I nodded, yes.

"I'm Harley, cousin to Josh and Nakiya. I'll be going to school here starting Monday. Josh asked me to come early and check on you, as I'm learning the healing arts of my clan and said you might need attention from your encounter with a bear."

"Oh, come in Harley. I only woke up a few minutes ago and haven't had a chance to look at them yet.

Whatever Josh gave me to sleep seemed to have knocked me out," I said. "How did you get in here, anyway?"

"That must have been the skullcap that helped you sleep. It works well for that purpose," he said and grinned. "Josh left the back door open, but locked your door. He didn't think you would have visitors."

He closed the door behind him and walked over to the gauze bag that sat on the note Josh had left behind. "Do you have something we can heat water in?" he asked.

"Yes, if you go down the hall and take a left the first swinging doors go into the kitchen. You can heat the water on the stove," I said.

"Okay, but you best stay down. Josh will have my medicine bag if you break any stitches open," Harley said walking out the door. Lying back down on the bed didn't hurt my feelings any. I wondered how I was going to heal fast enough to start school on Monday. Several minutes later Harley returned with a steaming cup which he set on the desk. Picking up the gauze bag which held the herbs he then steeped them in the hot water.

"After you drink all of this, I will make a poultice to put on your wound. It will help speed you're healing. I know the strength and the power you felt after the sun dance ceremony; however, none of my brothers would take on a full grown grizzly even after that."

"Believe me, that's not what I set out to do. It just sort of happened," I say. "You were there?" I didn't know how much Josh had told Harley, so I decided to play it by ear and not volunteer more information than necessary which seemed to be the stance with the people I was meeting. After steeping the herbs a few more minutes Harley handed me the cup to drink and waited until the bitter-sweet liquid had been drained completely. I shivered as the last of it flowed down my throat.

"Yes as I'm learning the healing ways of my people, I was with my father."

"Do all your remedies taste terrible?" I asked moving my pillow into a more comfortable position.

"I believe so. Then no one would take them when they're well and perhaps overdose. Another reason why we are chosen to be a healer is not everyone has the aptitude or the patience to learn all the herbs and how to use them."

"That makes sense why that gift is past down generation to generation. I seem to be getting sleepy again."

"That is good. It will hurt less when I take your bandages off and put the poultice on and then rewrap your injuries," Harley said. I watched him pick up a larger pouch and leave my room. I assumed he was going back to the kitchen.

"*Spirit Walker, you can relax you are in good hands. Sleep now,*" I heard Moon Dancer say. However, I was too sleepy to answer him.

My eyes opened slightly when I felt my covers drawn back and then my bandage removed. I gritted my teeth and my eyelids snapped opened as it felt like my skin was opened up again and images of the huge grizzly's paw tore into my flesh once more.

"It's alright Kerry, the crusted flesh had to be removed," said Harley. "This will make it feel better and by morning you will see and feel a big difference. Just relax now, sleep."

I relaxed as the hot poultice was placed over my wounds, and after a few seconds I felt the soothing heat sink into my raw flesh on my stomach. I didn't notice the pain as much on the two strips that Running Wolf had stitched. I listened to Harley chant and the beat led me into a deep sleep.

It was dark when later I floated above my body, curious of the form that lay upon the bed. Gliding to the window I stopped only a second to glance at Harley asleep in the over-stuffed chair. Passing through the window I saw three of my spirit animals waiting for me. I captured the image of the wolf in my mind and seconds later I was running on all fours alongside White Wolf, Red Tail Hawk and Night Eagle flew above us. The miles were eaten up under our paws. The ground we covered led us to a lone tepee a quarter mile from Wolf Talkers. We saw Dark Antelope's bloody body lying beside his campfire.

"Will he die White Wolf," I asked.

"No Spirit Walker. I have sent a dream to Nakiya and she should be here shortly with help," he responded.

"Why, Nakiya?" I asked adamantly. "Wonder if Shawgun is still around here. How can I protect her?"

"Calm yourself, this night she'll be in no harm as she comes with two other Shamans, Thunder Sky and Blue

Heron. Blue Heron is Harley's father, a gifted healer and spiritual leader in his clan. He will keep Nakiya safe," White Wolf responded. "Running Wolf needs to stay with his great grandfather as Wolf Talker will walk with the spirits this night. See the red circle around the campfire and Dark Antelope? This is how Shawgun was able to use Dark Antelope. As Dark Antelope's hatred toward you made him an easy target to take his will and be used by Shawgun."

"Come, Spirit Walker," Night Eagle spoke. "It is time to return."

Reluctantly I followed Night Eagle and White Wolf. The night sky was overcast and clouds were swelling into large black barrels in the west. By the time we reached the school the wind was howling, the clouds continued their roll east and it started to rain.

Entering my room I looked down at Harley's body still sprawled out over the chair and smiled, feeling a strong kindred spirit toward him. Knowing I was safe and that Nakiya would be too, eased my mind. The wounds I had left on Dark Antelope's body had left him unconscious. I doubted he would know who saved his life, at least tonight. Slowly I sank into my body that slept peacefully.

I felt someone rock my shoulder.

"Do you feel like eating, Kerry? Rachel's friend brought breakfast by and told me the other student that would be staying at the school would arrive sometime this afternoon. She also said that Rachael and John wouldn't be back as her brother had been hurt and Wolf Talker had entered the land of spirits. She asked if we would welcome him and show him around," Harley said setting the tray down on the desk. "How are you feeling?"

"Like I could eat a horse, but I need to make a phone call first," I said as I carefully pulled the covers back and sat up. Surprised that my side didn't hurt as it had the night before," I grinned at Harley. "I'm not as sore this morning."

"That's good. We still need to put one more poultice on later."

I shuffled to the phone, moving a fragment faster than I did yesterday. I was worried about the dream I'd had last night and that someone might have lost some cattle. I listened to the phone ring scrapping my toe back and forth over the hard wood floor waiting for someone to pick up.

"Rose Feather Outfitters."

"Danene, didn't expect you to be home," I said, disappointed that Jace hadn't answered the phone.

"Sorry I'm not who you wanted to talk to," she said laughing.

"No I didn't mean it that way. How did the trip go?"

"We sold out all the hunts for this year and several hunts for next year. Your photos of the powwow were a huge success. Had a lot of people wanting to know who took the pictures. I wouldn't be surprised if you received some calls to do some photo shoots and I'm talking about with some big corporations."

"I'm glad they had a good response for your trip."

"That's why I'm home early. Now who did you want to talk to since you've wounded my ego?" she asked and by her tonality she was smiling.

"Didn't mean to Sis, but is Jace close?"

"He just came out of Daisy's barn. Give him a minute to get in here. Are your friends still coming for Christmas?"

"As far as I know they are. What was the sparks between you and Josh?" I teased.

"I don't know what you're talking about."

"Sure you do Sis. You can't hide things from me. Christmas is going to be mighty interesting, is all I can say."

"Kerry! Here's Jace."

"What's the matter," Jace asked his voice tight.

"I just called to see how things are there?"

"They've been quite if you're referring to grizzly activity. How are things going with your shifting? Getting a handle on it yet?"

"It's coming along, Jace. Wolf Talker has past away and Nakiya and Josh are back in Browning."

"I'm sorry to hear that, Kerry."

"School starts on Monday. I've met another of my spirit animals, Night Eagle, an owl. How's Shadow? He's too far away for mind-speech."

"Shadow is fine. How long is it going to take for you to tell me what's happened there? Danene has gone outside so we can talk now."

Once I started to tell Jace what had happened so far it was like a dam burst and I didn't quit until it was all out.

"Do you need me to contact a doctor?" He asked concerned.

"No. Josh left me some herbs to take and Harley, Josh's cousin has put some kind of poultice on my wounds and they're healing quit rapidly, surprisingly. Harley will be going to school with me here and he is also learning to heal. His father Blue Heron is the shaman of their clan," I said and paused before I went on. "I was mostly worried about more killings."

"There hasn't been any that I know from last night. I haven't had calls from other ranchers this morning. But you give me a call in a few days so I know you're alright. And if anything happens here, I'll call you."

"Okay, Jace," I said and hung up the receiver feeling a little more relieved. I glanced at the big numbered clock that was framed in deer spikes hanging above the swinging doors to the class room. Twenty after nine, I'd slept longer than I thought. Our new arrival would be here this afternoon and I had so much I wanted to get done. Hearing the rumblings in my stomach I went back to my room to eat.

"Harley, do you know the other student who will be staying here at the school?" I asked sitting down at my desk. I uncovered my plate to find eggs, ham, hash browns and homemade biscuits with strawberry jam.

"If it's not hot enough I can go heat it up in the oven," Harley stated.

"No, its fine," I responded.

"His name is Roger Hopkins. He's father owns an outfitters in Utah. That's all Rachel's friend told me and that he'd be here later this afternoon," Harley said picking up his biscuit he had spread strawberry jam over. "After we finish eating we need to put another poultice on your wounds and then you should be in pretty good shape for school tomorrow."

"I really feel pretty good Harley, besides I have pictures I need to develop."

"Josh must know you well as that he told me you would want to rush things. Well, we'll see how you feel in a half hour or so," he said smiling and continued eating his breakfast.

I took my dish back to the kitchen, washed it and set it in the drainer, and then looked for a coke in the fridge. Rachel's friend had also stocked the fridge and I didn't know why I was surprised knowing that the students ate lunch here during the week. I took out a coke and returned to my room my eyes feeling heavy again. Harley was mixing the ingredients for the poultice when I walked in.

"Did you put something in my food to make me sleep again, Harley?"

"Like I said, Josh knows you pretty well. He said you would fight staying down so he left me some herbs to mix with your food as he didn't think I could get you to drink another cup."

"Darn him," I said making it to the bed before I thought my legs would give out from under me. I fought to keep my eyes open and the last thing I saw was Harley smiling and putting his mixture in a gauze bag.

Chapter SEVEN

"Kerry, wake up," Harley said while lightly shaking my shoulder. Looking around through squinted eyes I realized I'd slept another day away. "Class will start in three hours and you need to eat and I need to change your bandage. I'm sure there are things you want to do before you go to class."

"Did that other kid make it in last night?" I ask pushing the covers back and running my tongue over my teeth. My mouth felt like it was full of cotton. Ambling into the bathroom, I turned on the faucet and drank from my cupped hands; and then splashed cold water on my face. I sniffed again at the odor and realized it was me. It had been three, four days since I'd had a shower.

"Harley, can I cover this so I can take a shower? I can't go to class smelling like this," I stated wrinkling my nose. I watched him set the poultice down and pick up a black jar.

"I'll cover your side wounds with this and you can cover your stomach lacerations. A thin layer should work well enough if you keep the water a light spray. It's

118

healing quickly and one more poultice should do the job," he said smearing the honey like texture over my wounds. Finished with my side, he handed me the jar. "I'll be back in twenty minutes."

"I'll be out by then." After spreading the substance over my stomach I washed several times to remove it from my hands, and then gathered my clothes I'd be wearing today.

Feeling a little more human I walked over to the window hoping to see one or more of my spirit animals. They must be laying low. I sat down and carefully pulled my boots on as Harley walked back into my room.

"Impressive," he said. "I didn't think you'd be able to do that yet."

"Well, you know what they say; they grow'em tough in Montana," I grimaced as I sat back up and removed the towel from my lap. I didn't want to get the black goo on my jeans. "You didn't answer me about the kid from Utah."

"Yes. He and a Mr. Chavez arrived about the same time," Harley said placing the bowl with the hot poultice on the desk. "Mr. Chavez will be starting the class. John is in Browning with Rachel for the next few days. I don't know if they will name a Shaman right away. It will depend on the council and Wolf Talker's last instructions to them."

Even though I had met Wolf Talker in one of my dreams and at the powwow in Browning, the five days I spent in his lodge I felt I had known him forever. I guess with Moon Dancer's memories in my head that helped. Wolf Talker had given me wisdom I would carry with me always.

"Let's get this wrapped and then we'll go get something to eat. I wouldn't be surprised if Mr. Chavez is up and maybe Hopkins," Harley commented as he lifted the thin poultice out of the bowl and put it against my skin. Holding in place the gauze wrap Harley quickly taped it securely. I believed this stuff to be magic. I was sore but it was manageable. And after seeing my flesh torn apart that Wednesday night, it was hard for me to believe how good it looked now.

Walking through the swinging doors into the kitchen, Harley was right. Mr. Chavez and Roger were up, and making breakfast.

"Morning," I say walking up to the counter. "I'm Kerry McDaniels from Rose Feather Outfitters in Libby Montana. Sorry I wasn't up to meet you, I've been a little under the weather the last few days." I shook hands with both of them.

"John told me he had a photographer coming in early. I just thought you would be older the way he talked about your work," Mr. Chavez said cracking eggs into a bowl. "Have a seat. I was just fixing French toast and there's plenty to go around."

"That would be great," I replied looking over at Harley. He shook his head up and down and pulled up a chair.

"My name is Roger Hopkins, my family owns Pine Lodge Outfitters in Castle Dale, Utah. I believe I've seen your sister at some of the shows I've been to; long blonde hair, blue eyes, cuts a nice view in a pair of Levis, no offence," he said grinning.

"None taken. That would be my sister, Danene. She does all the shows for Rose Feather."

"I wish I had a sister like that, we might get more business. I've got five brothers and I'm the best looking," he said and started to laugh. "You take the pictures she has in her booth?"

"Yah. That's one talent she doesn't have." I say looking at him and then Mr. Chavez.

"Harley I didn't get a chance to ask you where you were from when we come in yesterday afternoon," Mr. Chavez said taking down the large fry pan hanging over the stove. We watched as he lit the burner.

"My tribe is up past the Canadian border," Harley replied.

"John scheduled ten students this session, and Kerry, you're the only one from Montana. The school is getting well known. You boys want to get a plate down from the cupboard. We have two hours before class and I have things I need to do before we start so I'll leave the clean up to you boys when we're finished eating."

"Sounds fair to me," I said and the others agreed.

When Harley and I walked into the classroom I was surprised how different it looked from the time John had taken me on a tour of the building. The tables were set in a U shape and in the middle of the U a small table stood, I supposed for the instructor. Ten manuals were placed equal distances around the tables along with a pencil and pad, a small knife and two sculpture tools. I understood now why there were no windows along the east wall. A cupboard ran the whole length of the wall. In the middle section a six by six foot portion was painted white. I was sure it was used with the projector.

There were models of different sizes on both sides and mounted on the wall a beautiful elk and a deer. Several birds and an eighteen inch rainbow trout were also mounted on the wall. Looking at them I wonder why John had needed photos. I guess I would learn later. The north and west sides had large windows which allowed the natural light into the room, but also blinds that could filter the light when needed. I didn't know how sunlight would affect the caps or if it did. The south wall there was a sink; counter space and what looked like a large freezer.

"Where do you want to sit Kerry?" Harley asked as he finished his own assessment of the room.

"How about here at the end of the table. We can see out the north and west windows and the lighting is still good," I said, "and besides we have a fast exit out and won't disturb anyone if one of us is a few minutes late."

We pulled up our stools and were looking at the manual as other students started to filter in. I was surprised the age difference in the group. I reckon I was thinking that they would all be around my age. I thought back to the two old timers that always occupied Mr. Granger's rocking chairs in front of his café. The stories they could tell. Though none in the class were that old, I imagined they would have bits of wisdom to pass down.

"Good morning gentlemen and welcome. Your head instructor John Monroe will be in later this week. I'm Mr. Chavez and have been an instructor here at the school the last sixteen years and have been doing Taxidermy for twenty seven. Please don't be shy about asking questions. I believe the only stupid question is the one not asked. Although I've been instructing for a long time I believe there is always more to learn. Please put your name on your manuals and your tools. If you lose them, the cost of a new one is posted in the hall. Lunch will be served at noon and we are privileged to have one of the best cooks in Havre, Mrs. Cottrell cooking for us. Now for introductions, please state your name, where you are from and why you are taking this class. We'll start at this end of the table."

I stood up and looked around the room before I gave my name and was glad to see that everyone had a friendly smile and hopefully one objective; to learn taxidermy. Roger was the only one I would have a problem with slipping away from at night, but time would tell.

"Howdy. My name is Kerry McDaniels from Rose Feather Outfitters out of Libby Montana. I want to learn taxidermy so we have another service to offer our clients," I stated and then sat back down on my stool.

"I'm Harley Otter from the Blackfoot Tribe near Del Bonita, Canada. Learning Taxidermy will bring in another source of income for my clan," Harley said looking down at the text book in front of him.

I was seeing another side of Harley. As competent as he was in treating my injuries, he was the opposite around other people; shy, reserved. The feeling we would become good friends was strong in me and he was someone I knew I could trust. As soon as Harley sat down a cowboy in his fifties stood up. His blue denim western cut shirt was accented with a red neckerchief. The wrangler jeans edged the bottom heel of his worn black boots and the shaped white straw hat set next to the cowboy's text book. From his eyes down he was suntanned, his forehead a dozen shades lighter. He twisted his mustache lightly before he spoke.

"Hi ya all. I'm Garrett Ritter from Sweetwater, Texas. I'm taking this class for a hobby. I have a lot of friends who like to hunt," he stated, giving us a toothy smile that would have done Texas proud.

"Roger Hopkins from Castle Dale, Utah and my family owns Pine Lodge Outfitters. And I'm taking the class the same as Kerry, to bring in another stream of income," he said looking over at me and nodded.

Roger was a couple of inches shorter than me and slightly stockier but you could tell he worked on a ranch or at least I could. His sleeves were rolled up and his forearms were well muscled from throwing hay bales and I bet he'd milked a cow or two. He liked socializing, as I had watched him mingle with the other class members before class. His friendly face and happy attitude I was sure was an asset to his family's business.

"I'm Brett Stocker from Colorado, Carl Adler from New Mexico and Aspen Higgins from Arizona," he said looking at each one of his friends as he said their name. "We all have shops in our own states. We met ten years ago at a work shop learning to make silver jewelry and became good friends. So every year one of us picks a class to expand our business, and this year was my turn."

I decided that Brett was the out-going of the three or so it seemed. At least he was the spokesmen this morning. Carl and Aspen smiled and nodded their heads in agreement. It seemed strange but the three could pass for brothers. All were about the same height and weight, dark hair and dark eyes. All three wore cowboy hats, each one a different shade of brown.

"Good morning, I'm Jake Wayland. Our family has an emporium in Jackson, Wyoming. I work with bronze and other metals. Father does taxidermy, but sometimes you need instruction from an outsider," he concluded and sat back down.

"I'm Nat Wayland and I do pottery and I paint landscapes. Father is going to retire in the next couple of years and he wants us to carry on his very successful taxidermy business. And as Jake mentioned sometimes it's easier to learn a skill from outside the family."

"This class will be very successful for you and you will be able to accomplish your goal for coming to this class. I received a message last night that a student cancelled, so there will only be the nine of you this session," Mr. Chavez announced. "How many of you have any knowledge of Taxidermy?"

Six of us raised our hands. What I knew had come from reading books. At the ranch we skinned the animals and sent them to a taxidermist two hundred miles away and the clients took it from there.

"All right, how many of you have had some kind of hands on experience?"

"Nat and I have helped our father put the capes on the models, but Dad has always done the rest," Jake stated.

"I've helped my sister tan hides to make into clothing. Nothing beyond that have I had experience," Harley commented.

No one else remarked as we looked at one another.

"Harley, you know how to do the most important part of taxidermy, tousling. If you don't know how to prepare your hide/cape you won't be happy with your finished product nor will your client. I want all of you to read the first chapter in your text book. It's only ten pages so it shouldn't take you that long and then it will be time for lunch," concluded Mr. Chavez. "Oh, before I forget, if you haven't noticed there is a pad under your text book. Please write down any questions when it comes to you. Thinking you'll remember the question later doesn't always work and it could make the difference between a good end product and a great end product."

I had questions but not for Mr. Chavez. I needed to talk to my spirit animals. I opened my text book and put one foot down on the floor to stretch my side. Being awake I was more aware of Harley's poultice taped to my side. The warmth had left and the tape pulled on my skin.

"What's the matter, Kerry? Harley whispered and stopped me from pressing my hand against my side. "At lunch time we'll take it off. Try and not touch it or it will irritate your skin."

I nodded and sat back up on my stool. Putting my note pad to the side I started to read the chapter on hide skinning. By the time I was finished I thought I would go crazy with the desire to scratch up and down my side and my stomach.

"Gentlemen, we'll be eating in the dining room which is through these doors and the first door to your right. Lunch will be served in fifteen minutes so if you would like to wash up, now would be the time."

Harley and I hurried past Mr. Chavez and back to my room before anyone else had a chance to stop us and chat. I took off my shirt as soon as I entered my room and went straight to the bathroom.

"Let me see before you try and take the bandage off," Harley insisted. "Do you want to lie down or stay standing while I do this? It's your choice. But I think it would be better if you lay down."

I didn't ask why looking at the gleam in Harley's eyes, but went over to the bed.

"If it's itching that's a good sign, Kerry," he said taking out a small jar from his medicine bag that was on my dresser. "Put your arm up over your head."

I looked down and watched his fingers slide along the tape. At two corners there was a small strip of black material Harley pulled up to get his fingers under and then pulled one side of the tape from my skin.

"Jeepers that hurts," I said gritting my teeth.

"Look! Out the window," he exclaimed and pulled the rest of the tape from my skin.

I just about come off the bed, and then I yelled into my pillow.

"Now that wasn't so bad, was it?" He said opening the jar. He spread some of the black goo where the tape had been and it felt soothing.

"Do I have any skin left," I asked trying to hold back the tears I felt escaping.

"It would have been worst if you had grown hair on your body as I've seen on other white men. You only have a small patch on your chest hardly noticeable."

I didn't know how to take that comment so I let it slide. I'd been excited when I'd started growing that small patch of hair.

"This salve will take away the pain and irritation on your skin where the tape was. Your stitches look good. I will be able to take them out the end of the week. Go look in the mirror. The lacerations on your stomach look like mere scratches now."

I took a quick look in the mirror. Harley was right, they were healing well and faster than anything I'd seen knowing the damage Zeal had done as that grizzly.

"We best get back, I'm hungry. Aren't you?" I asked. "Thank you, Harley." He smiled but said nothing and followed me out the door.

"Kerry, we've heard great comments on the hunts at Rose Feather," Jake said as he placed his plate down and pulled out the chair.

"We do our best," I said feeling a sense of pride.

"We also hear you have some of the finest horses. I have friends that purchased two fillies that brag about them all the time," Nat jumped in settling in the chair across from me.

"My dad and my brother Rob train our horses and we breed them at the ranch also. Rob says the breeding is as important as the training."

"We were thinking about getting one for our mom," Jake remarked.

"I would suggest you get a hold of Rob and let him know what you're looking for. He usually always has a waiting list for a Rose Feather horse."

"Isn't your sister Danene McDaniels?" Nate asked.

I chuckled to myself, as this was the second reference to my sister today.

"Yes. Danene does all our shows for us."

"Then are you the brother who takes all the photos she has in her booth?" Nat questioned.

"That would be me," I grinned.

"Would there be a chance we could contract you to do some photo shoots for us this winter in Jackson?" Nate asked. "You're photography is unbelievable."

"Thanks. I have some commitments already this winter," *like killing a demon.* "I'll have to get back with you, if that's alright. I can't promise anything right now." *Who knows if I'll still be alive?*

CHAPTER EIGHT

"This should be the last poultice we have to put on your wounds," Harley said putting the herbs into the hot water.

"I won't complain, Harley," I replied looking out my bedroom window.

"Spirit Walker, we have a journey to take tonight."

I heard Night Eagle say and then saw him perched on the corner on the roof.

"Where are we going?" I asked.

"To Browning, I will be back in an hour. You should be asleep by then," he said and flew off to the east.

"Kerry whenever you're ready. This is easier to put on if you lay down."

"Oh, yeah it does seem to work better going on or coming off when I lay down," I commented. "What did you think of class today?" I asked lying down on my bed and putting my arm up over my head.

"I liked it and specially Mr. Chavez. He has a laid back way of teaching that sets you at ease. The others in the class helped with their easy conversation," Harley said as he laid the poultice over my side and proceeded to tape it in place. "The looks on Aspen and Brett's faces were priceless when Mr. Chavez took the capes out of the freezer. Did you know they were kept in the freezer three to six months before they are worked?"

"I did not. We sent the hides to a taxidermist in Butte, Montana so what happened to them after that was between the taxidermist and the client. What does make me happy is that the animals I've photographed here weren't killed for this class," I said sitting up. "I'm really tired. I think I will turn in early tonight."

"That would be a good thing. It will give your body more time to do the final healing. The poultice can work very well, but when your body can go into a resting state it can work even better. That's why Running Wolf gave you the skullcap to make you sleep," Harley commented walking toward the door.

"Harley is your Indian name Otter?"

"Yes. That was the name given me; however the more we have done business with the whites I decided I needed a white name. A gentleman riding a motorcycle came into our shop and I asked him what kind of bike he was riding. I liked the style of the bike. He told me it was a Harley-Davidson. I liked the name Harley so I just added it to Otter."

"Well, I can't think of a better way of getting a name than picking it out yourself."

"Yah, that's what I thought. See you in the morning, Kerry," Harley said going out the door and then closed it behind him.

I heard the call of Night Eagle and I left my body.

"Where are we going?" I asked as we moved above the building.

"We're going to Browning," replied Night Eagle. "We will see what is taking place."

Moving beside Night Eagle was as unusual as the copper colored full moon that was leisurely making its way across the dark azure sky. The air was still. I hesitated looking down below but seemed compelled to look at the objects shadowed, reminding me of Icebis and things hidden. It's strange how night can swallow up the same terrain giving it an eerie feeling without changing a hill or bush. Shadows growing into whatever your imagination can conceive lingered below. Off to my right I saw Crow traveling with us.

"Night Eagle says your wounds are healing well with the help of Otter," Crow remarked.

"Yes. He must have magic in with the herbs he uses. I don't know how the rips in my skin could of healed this fast."

"We will continue your training later this week. We can't let too much time lapse until you are solid in shifting from one form to another," Crow said.

Hovering over Wolf Talker's teepee, we saw below thirty or so Blackfoot. Inside the teepee I saw Nakiya and Running Wolf along with their parents. Sub chiefs I'd met at the powwow in August; Elkhorn, Laughs-A-Lot and Wind Stepper, but I did not see Dark Antelope. There was one who was speaking I did not recognize.

"That is Blue Heron, Harley's father," Night Eagle spoke.

"He is wise and an excellent healer," stated Crow. *"He has taught his son well."*

We descended to where we could hear him speaking. Nakiya and her mother were crying as tears were running down their cheeks, yet as we drew closer they were speaking quietly in the Blackfoot language.

"One of our Great Shamans has departed from our earthbound existents'. He has always taught us wisdom and kept us close to the Creator. His skills he has passed down to his great grandchildren continuing his line since the days of Raven Feather and before."

I remembered that Moon Dancer had talked about his father Raven Feather. It had been only few days after I had learned that Moon Dancer shared my soul and for a time, my body and mind. And he would continue to do so until we found Moon Dancer's other stolen gift.

"While we continued to communicate Wolf Talker and I," continued Blue Heron setting Wolf Talker's pipe on his lap, "talked of who would succeed him after he journeyed on to the land of spirits. Being the wise Shaman that he was he brought many issues to these discussions, and he mentioned counseling with Elk Horn, Laughs-A-Lot, Wind Stepper and Dark Antelope. Our world is changing and to survive we must change with it and yet still hold on to our tradition and teach them to the generations to come. Since Dark Antelope is not with us we can…" He stopped for a moment and looked up.

I glanced to my left and saw Wolf Talker smiling at me.

"Moon Dancer wake up. You're son is here beside me. Moon Dancer!" I urged calling him from sleep in the back of my mind.

"Wolf Talker it is good to see you once more," I said hoping he could hear me.

"Spirit Walker here you are again among the spirits," he said, his smile widened. *"Blue Heron is keeping his promise to me as I listen to him speak. You and I will have to leave shortly so let's listen."*

I nodded and looked back to Blue Heron.

"He has asked you to consider both his great grandchildren take his place. Running Wolf who has walked among the whites and has kept his people the highest priority and whom Wolf Talker passed down the sacred arrows and the gifts given him by his father, Moon Dancer. Nakiya who has also walked in the white man's world and the knowledge she has learned she has brought back to her people. This is his request Wolf Talker has ask me to present to you," he said looking around the teepee at the elders present."

Watching the expression on Nakiya's face this had come as a surprise to her, however as usual Running Wolf showed no expression. He sat next to Wind Stepper his head turned toward Blue Heron as though his name hadn't been mentioned.

"My great grandson will become an exceptional Shaman and you Spirit Walker will bring great honor to the Blackfoot people," spoke Wolf Talker.

"Spirit Walker, tell my son I will see him soon," said Moon Dancer. *"And that I am proud of him."*

I relayed the message and turned back to the conversations below.

"*It is time we left, Spirit Walker. We have one more stop before we return home*," Night Eagle said and guided me away.

I wanted to protest until we heard the council's decisions; however we were already heading in another direction. We stopped at the camp of Dark Antelope where herbs hung around the entrance to his teepee and a shaman who I didn't recognize was chanting. John and his wife Rebecca sat on the other side of Dark Antelope. Rebecca was holding his hand and I noticed several herb bracelets around both his wrist.

"He has a high fever from your wolf bite, but his mental state is weak from being used by the demon Shawgun. The herbs you see at the entrance will keep Shawgun out. This Shaman is well versed for the mental state Dark Antelope is in. It's Rebecca who will heal his physical ailments. Come, we must go back to the school now," Night Eagle stated.

"Will he recover and will Shawgun be able to use him again?" I asked following him.

"He will recover from his wounds, but I don't know the answer to your last question," he responded.

A knock on my door roused me from a deep sleep. Groggy I went to the door, unlocked the catch and opened it up. I was surprised to see Roger and not Harley standing in the door way.

"When you sleep, you sleep deep. This is the third time we have tried to rouse you," He said. "Your breakfast is getting cold."

"Sorry. I'll be out in a few minutes." I shut the door and made it half way to the bathroom when there was another knock. "Come in Harley," I said and continued to the bathroom.

"You feeling all right Kerry?" Harley asked shutting the door behind him.

"I guess I was just really tired. How late am I?"

"You've got time to shower and eat. Let me look at your side first. Your stomach looks like mere scratches; however I think we need to cover your side a day or two more. How's your side feeling?"

"It's feeling a lot better, Harley. You've done a great job. I can't wait to tell Josh how good a job you've done. I still can't believe it sometimes when I look in the mirror."

"I wished I could have saved you from having the scaring you're going to have but I think as you get older it will fade."

Mr. Chavez raised his eyebrows when we walked into the kitchen but didn't say a word however he did look at his watch before he left.

"Guess I didn't make any points this morning," I said looking at Harley and then Roger.

"If you hurry we won't be late for class," Harley returned.

"I'll see you guys. I'm going in. I want to talk to Mr. Chavez before class starts," stated Roger.

We both nodded and I picked up a plate and Harley poured us each a glass of milk. I jumped when the toast popped up in the toaster nearly losing my eggs to the floor.

"When you need to talk you let me know," Harley said buttering the lightly colored bread, and then placed them on my plate. "I'm going into class and I suggest you hurry.'

My eyes followed Harley until he disappeared through the swinging doors. If only I could ask Moon Dancer if it was safe to talk to Harley. Having Shadow to talk to at home made me realize how much I missed him. Tonight I would find my spirit animals and ask them to give me their opinion. I finished eating and placed my plate in the sink and quickened my steps to class.

"I'll bet you were surprised that wearing animal skins dated back to Adam and Eve. But it was the Egyptians, Greeks and Romans that contributed much to the science of skin tanning. The Native Americans were well versed in the art of tanning and taught the pioneers the process of soft buckskin tan which even today has scarcely been improved upon. Did anyone have any question on chapter one?" asked Mr. Chavez waiting for someone to speak up. When no one commented he continued.

"It's relatively easy to skin a bird and that is what we will be doing first. I listed on a piece of paper those birds that were attained last week for class. You will be doing two in this class, so I suggest that you pick the one that is your second choice to do first. Look at the list and mark the two you want to do. Put your name on the paper and I'll have Roger collect them.

"What form are you going to use Harley?" I asked. Opening my manual I scanned over the first chapter again. I was feeling pretty confident that whatever I picked I'd just use my gift and have it finished in no time at all.

"A quail, if they have one."

"Hum. I hope they have a red tail hawk. That is what I want to do," I sported. "Yes, a red tail hawk I want to do but for my second one only." *That was an excellent choice since I had one for a friend.*

"After you've given Roger your paper, open your manual and read chapter two."

"Mr. Chavez," Aspen said opening his manual. "We're only going to do two projects?"

146

"You'll find as beginners, Aspen, you want to be off to a fast start, however, proceeding slowly and patiently you will be satisfied more with the end result. We will only have time to do two in this class even with two instructors," he replied.

"That's right; John will be back Friday if everything went well," I said to Harley.

"I wonder if they have chosen a new Shaman?" Harley questioned.

"I don't know. If they choose Josh or Nakiya how will that affect what they are doing now? Josh is just about done with veterinarian school and Nakiya is supposed to start school in Chicago mid-winter."

"Kerry whatever the outcome many prayers and discussions will have gone into making the decision. Wolf Talker last wishes will hold a heavy vote, as he knows the people of his clan. It's something we'll have to wait and see. They might even hold off for a short while."

"Would Zeal/Dark Antelope have a determining factor?"

"Since he is on the council, they may wait for him to vote. Again, we'll have to wait and see." We turned to chapter two in our manuals and started reading, though my focus wasn't on the page.

Sliding my window open, I slipped through and jogged up toward the ravine. A white halo emerged and I knew it was my spirit animals and I picked up my pace. Neither my side nor my stomach gave me any grief.

"Spirit Walker it is good to see you in your physical form," Crow said flying to meet me and then landing on my shoulder strap of my backpack.

"It's good to see you all." Coming to a stop in front of White Wolf, Great Bear and Fox," I asked. "Would telling Otter compromise anything?"

"Why do you ask? What does your heart tell you?" Asked White Wolf.

"My heart says that we'll become great friends and it's hard not having anyone to talk to."

"And so you will. Otter is on the path to becoming a great shaman like his father. Shadow and Jace have always been your confidants, however they are not here. I see no reason why you cannot confide in Otter," replied White Wolf.

Looking at the others, they were also in agreement with White Wolf. I felt better that my own judgment had been a good one concerning Otter.

"Friday, Otter says he will take out my stitches, and then I can practice shifting again."

"That will be good Spirit Walker. Until shape-shifting comes to you like the air you breathe it's not good to go so long without practicing," Crow said.

"In your taxidermy you need to have patience. A pine tree was not grown overnight, nor will your ability. It will take much practices as your shape-shifting," Great bear stated.

"But I have my gift."

"As always you are in such a hurry," commented Great Bear. "Enjoy the journey for it will give you the greatest joy."

After saying good night to my spirit animals I walked back to my room. I wondered how much my gift would help me if it was going to take me the same amount of time as it did everyone else. I had learned to talk to the animals quickly when I photographed them, why wouldn't this be the same.

CHAPTER NINE

Friday after noon John walked into the class room. He talked to Mr. Chavez for a few minutes before Mr. Chavez had us stop what we were doing.

"Class I'd like to introduce John Monroe owner of the school and also an instructor. I'd like you to introduce yourselves starting with you Aspen and we'll go around the room.

"It's nice to put names to faces. I've been told by Mr. Chavez you've had a productive week," John said laying the large album down on the center table. In this album there are step by step pictures of different birds and ducks you can look at. Also in the back there are pictures taken a couple of weeks ago by Kerry McDaniels at my request. I think you'll enjoy looking at them, also. I won't keep you from your day's schedule and I will see you Monday morning." Moving toward the door he stopped for a moment in front of my model and spoke softly.

"Kerry I need to speak to you tonight. I'll come back around seven to pick you up," he said and left the room through the double doors.

I smiled and nodded and continued working on my model. I marked the points on the cord-wrapped excelsior where the wings and tail would attach. Spun a sufficient amount of cotton batting on the neck wire and wrapped it in place with the cord to form the neck. I found reading out of a book was totally different than hands on. But then I thought it would be easier. I was going to have to work as hard at this as I did at shape-shifting.

As I cut the wire twice the length for a leg, I thought tonight would be a good time to tell Harley what was going on with Shawgun. I surmised it would be wiser to let him know when I was leaving and what for, so if Roger come looking for me after bedtime I'd have an ally. Roger seemed to stick to us like glue. I'm sure it was because we were both from an outfitter and the three of us were staying at the school, but sometimes I felt suffocated and we'd only been going to school a week. He was going to be harder to slip away from than I thought.

I decided to have my birds wings spread out so I was going to have to insert the wire at the wing tips, draw it through underneath, within the skin opening and out to the end of the upper-arm bones. I was concentrating so hard I hadn't seen Roger walk up beside me.

"Kerry," Roger sounded.

"Ouch," I murmured when I stuck my finger with a wire.

"Sorry. I didn't mean to scare you," Roger chuckled. "I just wanted to ask you if you wanted to go into town tonight with me, Aspen, Carl and Brett."

"Can't tonight I have some things I need to take care of. But thanks for asking, Roger."

"If you need some help I can stay," he said looking deflated.

"No, you go ahead. You could bring me back a package of snickers." Reaching into my pocket I retrieved a couple of dollars. "If you don't mind," I said giving him the money.

"Sure, I can do that," he said putting the money in his pocket.

Since it was Friday night Mr. Chavez ended class at four o'clock and everyone was ready leave. I didn't know what kind of night life Havre had, but I'm sure I would hear about it in the morning. As Harley and I walked down the hall I decided it was time to share a few things with him.

"Harley do you want to grab a sandwich with me and then we'll go to my room? I have some things I'd like to share with you."

"I am hungry and I saw Mrs. Cottrell bring in some fresh strawberries. If we're lucky she bought some cream, also," he said pushing through the swinging doors.

I stood looking out my window trying to decide where to start when I saw Crow land on my window sill.

"I always found that the best place to start is at the beginning," Crow suggested. *"Harley Otter knows things of the spirit."*

"Harley I guess the best place to start is at the beginning, my spirit animal Crow suggest that would be best."

"If you would call me by my native name during this time I will call you by yours, Spirit Walker. Crow is also one of my spirit animals, and it is wise to listen to him. He has been my guide since I was a small child."

I glanced at the clock, it read four forty five. That should be enough time before John comes to pick me up. So I started. Harley sat cross-leg on the floor and listened without interruption until I finished. We both sat in silence for a few more minutes before Harley said.

"Spirit Walker you have been a legend among my people for three generations. Moon Dancer was a great warrior and shaman and the legend began when he saved his sister Spotted Fawn from being a blood sacrifice from the demon skin-walker Shawgun. His bravery, courage and faith in the creator let him escape many traps the demon set for him throughout his life. When he passed over and Shawgun stole his gifts the earth shook and my people mourned," Otter said walking over to the window where Crow still perched on the window sill.

"Through visions to my Great-great grandfather He Who Sees Spirits, he saw what would happen when Moon Dancer made his last try into his shaman linage. He knew when Moon Dancer's soul entered into the body of a white child. He Who Sees Spirits was given a promise that the white child would shelter Moon Dancer's soul. That the child would walk in both worlds and his talents and gifts would be known to man and he would help the Blackfeet people. He also said his bloodline would mingle with ours. These visions have been past down. Many of the elders have waited for you to awaken and fulfill your destiny."

"That's pretty heavy stuff to lay on somebody Otter," I said swallowing hard.

"Not somebody, Spirit Walker, YOU!"

"He speaks true," Crow stated. *"You've heard a journey of a thousand steps begins with one. You've taken those first steps and you have a long journey ahead."*

I walked back over to the window and stood beside Otter. We looked out over the waving grasses of the prairie. I recalled the words that he said my blood would mingle with theirs. Does that mean that Nakiya and I would be together, knowing that's not where my thoughts should be focused, but my heart beat faster any way. My thoughts were interrupted by a knock on the door. Otter moved silently across the room and then opened it. I knew it would be John.

"Hello Otter. I see you two have become friends." He didn't wait for an answer. "You can come with us Otter."

I smiled, grabbed my hat and followed them out; closing and locking my door behind me.

"How has class been going and have you made friends with the other students," John inquired.

"Garret has a dry sense of humor and I find myself smiling inward a lot, where Aspen is just plain funny," I stated.

"Kerry has acquired a shadow," Otter chuckled. "Roger Hopkins. Well I haven't quite figured him out, but he does like to stay close to Kerry. The others are friendly and I'm learning a lot about different crafts when we have lunch."

We drove up to the ranch house and before John stopped the truck I notice two new horses in the corral.

"Nice horses," I commented.

"Yes they are. Zeal gave them to his sister when we left."

"He's recovering from his wounds, I take it?"

"You knew about them?" John asked turning the truck off.

"Yes," I said and got out of the truck without further explanation. Rachael was standing by the door. She was wearing a long colorful skirt and a maize blouse with turquoise moccasins that I'd bet she made herself.

"Hello Otter, how are you Kerry, or should I call you Spirit Walker away from school," she asked. I felt like I was on soggy ground not knowing what she knew or felt after being with Zeal.

I smiled and would let her call me what she thought was appropriate. I would listen to them before I made any comment and would follow Otter's lead if I felt uncomfortable. I was getting tired of feeling like I was walking on egg shells wondering who knew what and what I should talk about.

What happened to the easy life style I was use to? Sometimes I felt the world was resting on my shoulders and when Moon Dancer slept most the time I felt alone. Did he sleep to conserve his energy, remembering how tired we felt on Icebis being in his younger body? If he was conserving that was okay if it meant being full charge when the time came to hunt down Shawgun.

"I made brownies would you like some with some milk?" she asked going into the house.

We sat around the kitchen table with a large plate of brownies and tall glasses of cold milk. You'd think I'd be relaxed but I felt the tension building in the room the longer we munched.

"You both know that Wolf Talker has gone to the land of spirits. He left his desires known with the Elders about the next shaman but before he closed his eyes he passed the sacred arrows to Running Wolf his great grandson."

"Did the council not name the next shaman?" Otter asked looking at John and then Rachael.

"What you don't know," she said skirting around the question, "is that my brother Dark Antelope was attacked and nearly died. If it hadn't been for Blue Heron, evil spirits would have taken him," Rachael stated as tears slid down her cheeks she quickly wiped them away. "The council will not make a final decision until Dark Antelope can cast his vote."

"There was talk that Wolf Talker wanted both Running Wolf and Nakiya to share the responsibilities, and there has been much discussion among the elders. I heard say that Nakiya has given up many of their traditions," said John.

"Knowing what little I do about Nakiya she is learning different ways to help her people," I spoke up. "Going to school to be a vet gives Josh knowledge to help his people with their livestock. Does not a shaman work? Times have changed so much with your people Rachael; he has to be able to make a living."

"This is true Spirit Walker. But it is different for a man. If Nakiya is to share in a shamans duties as her great-grandfather requested she would have to hold on to the traditions. One would be honoring her parent's promise of giving her in marriage to Dark Antelope," Rachael remarked and looked right at me as if she were talking only to me.

Before I exploded into a verbal volcano of why she couldn't marry Dark Antelope, I felt Night Eagle's calming presence and his soft command to hold my tongue. I gripped the seat of my chair with both hands and still tried to act calm. When Otter looked at me and gave me a slight nod of his head I knew I wasn't doing a very good job. So when Rachael stood up and went into the kitchen I took that time to take a deep breath and slowly let it out and released the white knuckle grip I had on the chair. I let Night Eagle's serenity slowly seep into my body.

"I'm sorry Kerry," John said, concern written on his face. "I know how you feel about Nakiya. We both know that Zeal will agree with the council if not demand it if she wants to adhere to her Great-grandfather's wishes. She has been taught since she was young that one day, she would follow after him in the ways of the shaman."

"I'm hoping it won't be too long before Dark Antelope will have his full strength back. Whatever attacked him nearly killed him, and since Nakiya brought the Shamans to his aid I believe she saw her destiny with Dark Antelope and saved his life," Rachael said holding a sack in her hands. "That is what I wanted to tell you Spirit Walker. Whatever destiny you have it will not be with Nakiya. I know they say you are the legend that generations have whispered about around the campfires. If what they say is true you have your own destiny to consider and another path to follow."

She sat the sack on the table and pulled her white shawl tighter around her shoulders.

"I wanted you to hear this from John and I as we consider you a friend.

I have baked you and Otter some pastries to take with you. And Otter your father says he will speak with you soon and hopes you are enjoying your class. I'll say goodnight now."

Rachael hadn't given Otter or me the opportunity to open our mouths before she left the room. We all stood there for a few moments digesting what she had told us.

"Come boys I'll take you back to the school," John said and walked back outside in way of the kitchen. I picked up my hat, and Otter picked up the sack that Rachael had set on the table before we followed John.

"Rachael hasn't been herself since we come back from Browning. Zeal is her only blood relative alive and the way she almost lost him took a toll on her."

"John, did Zeal tell you what happened to him?" I asked.

"He didn't say anything to me and Rachael hasn't said if Zeal told her what really happened that I know of. I do know that Blue Heron and the other two shamans that were with him battled most the night against dark spirits to keep Zeal here. Why?"

"I was just curious." *I knew when Crow sent her to help him something would happen.*

"What do you boys have planned for the weekend?"

"I was going to take some more photos. Did you have something planned or were you going to come with me, Harley?

"I thought I'd tag along and watch you do your magic," Harley remarked.

"And what about Roger?" John asked.

"He went into town with Aspen, Carl and Brett. He didn't say if he was coming back tonight or tomorrow. I guess it depends on what activity they find in town tonight.

Listening to him I don't think he gets out a whole lot."

"I'll check in on him tomorrow. Then see if he wants to come out to the ranch for the day," John said. "Kerry did you know Wolf Talker for a long time?"

"No, why?" I asked looking out into the night.

"Before Wolf Talker passed over he asked Running Wolf to look after Spirit Walker. You're the only one I know by that name and the way he said it sounded like he knew you for a long time."

"Hum," I continued looking out the window a few moments before I answered. "That's strange as I only met him in person at the powwow."

"Yes, I thought it odd, also. It seemed to disturb Rachael; however she wouldn't talk about it. I was curious and since she hasn't been the same since she helped take care of her brother.

"Perhaps it is the loss of her clan's shaman and the worry over her brother," offered Harley. "Many things are changing as we try to adapt to the white man's world and still hold on to who we are."

"I'm sure your right Harley. Living here in Havre, Rachael has blended in with the community but Zeal holds tight to tradition. It must be a struggle for her."

"We'll see you on Monday. I think we may spend the night out under the stars," I said as the truck came to a stop and then Harley and I got out.

"In the back of the form room you'll find some sleeping bags, if you decide to do that.

Good night."

Roger's parking spot was still vacant so I assumed he was still in town. I didn't wait until John drove away to go inside.

"Night, Harley." And I slipped into my room. I couldn't hold back the tears any longer and I felt hollow. Thinking of Nakiya with Zeal made me feel like my heart was being ripped out. Even though she had no feelings for Zeal she would honor her Grandfather's wishes and it scared the crap out of me. Shawgun had used Zeal already, so what's saying he wouldn't do it again? Shawgun could use Zeal to get to Nakiya and complete the blood sacrifice he started so many years ago when he had taken Spotted Fawn and Moon Dancer had stopped him.

How could I stop him? I lay down on my bed and pulled the blanket over me. I couldn't dream of them that could start another killing spree back home. I can't sleep, I can't sleep.

Chapter TEN

"Spirit Walker, sleep dreamless, dreamless…" I heard Crow say softly.

We made sandwiches for lunch and would stop in Chinook for breakfast as the sun hadn't risen over the hills. It was Harley's suggestion we leave before daylight to avoid any entanglements with Roger as Harley had heard him come in late last night.

We were in our own thoughts watching the morning light roll up the night sky. We watched critters greeting the new day and I wondered what adventures it would bring to them.

We had turned onto highway 2 before either of us spoke and then it was Harley that broke the silence.

"If you want to practice your shape-shifting I know of a place that we can go and we won't see a soul. There's also a lot of game to capture with your camera."

"I've never tried to shape-shift in front of anyone other than my spirit animals, I don't know if I can or not," I stated.

"Your spirit animals will not always be around when you need to shift so this would be a good time to try, however, I believe wherever we stop your spirit animals won't be far away." Harley smiled.

"Harley, can you shape-shift?"

"Shape shifting is not one of my talents. If I have that ability it has not yet surfaced and my father has said nothing to encourage me to try."

"I didn't know I could until a few weeks ago and if the truth be known I don't think I was intended to shape-shift either. Swallowing that globe changed things for me."

"We do not know what the Creator intended. I have found in the small time I've been opening my talents with the spirits no one knows the paths the Creator will send you down. He doesn't always give us a road map to follow, but he is always with us to prompt us if we are in tune with him."

"Aren't you afraid sometimes Harley, walking with the spirits?"

"Yes, at one time I was. But I've learned my fear only gave the dark spirits more power, as fear feeds and strengthens them. As long as I do not fear them they cannot harm me. Some think the dark side is stronger, but it is not."

We turned onto a dirt road and followed it four or five miles. As Harley had mentioned we saw different types of game. Cresting a knoll we saw two young bucks sparing.

"Stop here Harley, I'd like to capture that scenario," I said opening the door as the truck come to a halt. With camera in hand I slowly made my way toward them.

"*Hello there,*" They stopped and looked around looking for the voice they heard.

"*Can I capture your sparing on film?*" I asked continuing down toward them. They turned toward me and the biggest spike took a few steps toward me, his head held high.

"You must be Spirit Walker are you not?" the spike asked.

"Yes, I am Spirit Walker."

"Your name precedes you. You are highly respected in our world by those that have met you. It would be an honor for you to photograph us."

"No the honor is mine," I responded stepping closer to the spot that would give me the best light advantage. *"Whenever you are ready."* Putting the lens to my eye I watched the show begin and clicked away. When the spikes stopped they bowed and I returned their bow with one of my own.

"I thank you and so do the many that will look upon these pictures." They both smiled before they turned and walked proudly into the buck-brush.

"Impressive. You honor them and your talent. Come we are not far from where we will make camp."

We rode another mile before Harley pulled up to the first patch of trees we'd seen since we left the highway. I saw the fire-pit that had been made from stones before stepping out of the truck.

"I take it you have been here before," I asked taking my gear out.

"Many times I come here to meditate and practice things my father has taught me. My spirit feels free and at peace here."

"I know what you mean. I felt that way at the summit. That was the second place White Wolf took me back in time, when Moon Dancer walked the earth."

"At the top of the line of trees there is a natural spring and it flows year round," Otter said taking a bundle of firewood from the truck bed along with one of the sleeping bags.

I put my camera in the cab and then pulled out the other sleeping bag from the back. I put it down not far from Otters.

"What do you think about before you shift," he asked.

"I try to think of something small like a squirrel or a prairie dog when I've tried at the school. I didn't want to damage the furniture. When I'm out it's usually a wolf. I feel more comfortable in that form."

"I would think you would since it was the white wolf that started you on this journey. But the wolf you freed from the trap I believe was sizing you up to see if you were ready to start this journey."

"Yes I feel close to White Wolf, however Shadow, my dog is one of my spirit animals. Shadow is my best friend. And since we can mind speak that has made us closer. You'd think Otter, that I would shape-shift into a dog instead of the wolf."

"You have seen the wolf in spirit form and it is easier for you to grasp that. Shadow is like another human to you."

"That's a very good analogy, Otter," said White Wolf. "Your father should be proud of your growth."

"White Wolf, I'm so glad you're here," I said going to stand in front of him.

"Are you ready to shape-shift again," Great Bear said appearing along with Night Eagle and Crow.

"I know what you're thinking Spirit Walker," Night Eagle remarked. "But I promise it will be no different with Otter here."

I looked over at Otter and smiled. "You won't laugh at me will you, Otter."

"I may laugh with you, but never at you, Spirit Walker. I'm just going to go sit over here and if I can help, say so. Otherwise I will be an observer."

"Fair enough. Okay, I'm ready," I said looking around me to make sure nothing would be in my way.

"Think of the animal you want to shift into." I heard Crow say.

I saw the wolf and pulled back. Thinking of my side being ripped open I automatically pulled my belly in and my fingers traced the two scars on my side.

"Relax Spirit Walker; no one is here but us. Try again, but start with something smaller," White Wolf coached.

I strained for a rabbit as I pushed the fear behind me. I saw the long ears, the soft fur, hard toenails and the wisp of whiskers around the nose. My vision blurred as I was now on my hands and knees. I felt my bones reshaping… *Oh the pain*, it rushed through me and I pulled back again my sides heaving like a jack hammer and sweat dripped from my forehead.

"May I," Otter asked approaching my spirit animals. They must have agreed because the next thing I knew Otter was standing beside me with his hand on my shoulder.

"Spirit Walker if you fail to shape-shift Shawgun has won half the battle. He has made your fear like a brick wall. Each time you pull back another layer of brick is put in place. He's hoping you will build the wall so high you won't even attempt it."

"Otter I see that bear coming at me and feel the pain all over again," I said lifting my head up to look at him.

"That is exactly what he wants, Spirit Walker. I suggest to you that stopping your shape-shifting must be very important to Shawgun. Consider this, if Shawgun succeeds to cowering you to shape-shift and he's successful in kidnapping Nakiya, what will stop him from sacrificing her. If your ability to shape-shift was the difference between her living and dying and you knew that in your heart…"

"I see your point, I'll try again."

"No Spirit Walker. Do not try. Do or do not," stated Great Bear.

I took a deep breath to slow my breathing and brought the wolf back into my mind. I felt my jaw elongate and my teeth lengthen. Looking at my hands fur broke out between my knuckles, fingers retracted and I was standing on paws. Bones felt like they were breaking and rearranging as I guess they were. I cringed trying not to hold on to the pain and held back my tears.

It won't be long, I kept thinking. Finally looking through yellow eyes my sight changed and when I sniffed I smelled scents that were further out than I could see. My hearing was acute to the smallest sounds around us. I lay on my belly looking at the others through my wolf eyes.

"You have a beautiful black and silver pelt."

I heard Otter say as he sat motionless waiting to see what I would do next. The strange sensation of being able to understand him and yet be in this form amazed me. I wondered if Otter could mind speak? I looked at him and said, *"Thank you, Otter."*

His eyes widened. *"I guess that is a talent you didn't know you had. Can you only hear me, or can you answer me as well?"* I felt like I had static going through my mind. Had it been that way when I started to talk to

Shadow? *"Whoa. Slow down and say just one or two words to begin with slowly,"* I said with a toothy grin. *"Crow did you know that Otter had this gift?"*

"Our gifts are meant to be found when we need them, and yes I knew that his mind speech lie dormant. I'm sure that Blue Heron will be happy that it has been discovered."

Standing up I trotted along the tree line. Before I ventured further I looked to the horizon and sniffed the air. Satisfied I was safe I loped and then burst into a run relishing the freedom I felt. Coming to a halt I sat on my hunches for a moment as I decided what animal I would test this new freedom on. I thought of Red Tail Hawk who I hadn't seen for a week. I captured the bird's essence and I was flying. What a rush looking down on everyone as the current carried me across the meadow.

"Spirit Walker," called Otter. I came to land a few feet from Otter starting the change back. The exhilaration must have camouflaged the pain when I changed into the hawk because now I felt ever bone and muscle as my body reshaped back into me. I fell to the ground in a fetal position and held my sides.

"Deep slow breaths Spirit Walker. This will happen for a while, however the pain won't last long," White Wolf said his paw on my shoulder. The pain seemed to be leaving through my shoulder and then I realized that White Wolf was drawing the pain away.

"White Wolf, Crow, will Shawgun kill tonight since I've been able to shape-shift? Will he retaliate? I'm afraid for those at home."

"Relax your shape-shifting has been shielded," Crow answered. *"I wouldn't try shifting again until tomorrow, your body needs to rest. Tomorrow decisions will be made in Browning. And you Spirit Walker will need to keep your focus on your goal. Even though Moon Dancer sleeps he is weakening, you cannot conquer Shawgun alone and Moon Dancer knows this. Recovering the last gift has to be your priority. We are going now as you and Otter will have a lot to talk about."*

"Come Spirit Walker and bring your camera. Do you believe that words flow easier when your feet are moving forward?

"I do," I said picking up my camera and slipping the strap around my neck. I saw that Otter had picked up the backpack with our sandwiches. "Lead on," I smiled and took a step behind him.

"When you were a child Spirit Walker, were there other things that made you seem different from others?" Otter asked stretching out his stride up the knoll.

There were a few white fluffy clouds to the west that would play hide and seek with the sun later in the afternoon. The trail we trekked snaked around sage and buck brush. The wild roses and rabbit brush had lost most their flowers and the green wheat grass was turning golden.

"I believe that after the episode with my school friends, if there was to be any abnormal activity I blocked any chance of it coming forward. I didn't want to be different. I never let my mind follow the unusual."

"I can understand that. Especially having no guidance or anyone to ask questions," Otter sympathized with Spirit Walker realizing how alone he must have felt being different. "My father has always been there and encourages me to explore the talents that come to me."

"Sometimes Otter I felt my Mom knew things and though she feared for me, she never prohibited me from experiencing the unknown. Running Wolf said she had precognitive abilities.

If she has other talents I don't think anyone was there to help her. One day when the hunt for Shawgun is over I will have to sit down with my parents and let them in on a few things. But being parents and specially my dad, right now he'd try and stop me not knowing what the consequence might be," Kerry stated lengthening his own stride.

"I see the fear in my mother's eyes when I open up a new gift in my mind, but she has kept silent. However I have heard them speak when they didn't know I was around. My mother has spoken her mind with my father and in his wisdom he has let her vent. And in the end she follows him and accepts the trials I must endure to walk in my father's footsteps," Otter said with pride in his voice.

"Spirit Walker, come with me," Night Eagle called.

Leaving my body I left it there beside Harley Otter who slept soundly. Rising into the air, again I saw Crow waiting for me and Night Eagle. I didn't ask questions feeling the wind race through my hair as we traveled west.

My perception was we were traveling toward Browning and hopefully to Nakiya.

Hovering above the old shaman's teepee it felt strange being able to see inside where Running Wolf and Nakiya and her parents were talking.

"Nakiya the decision has to be yours. Sometimes we as parents do things in the heat of the moment. Dark Antelope's mother and I were best friends and you were still an infant when your father and I agreed to the promise between you and Dark Antelope. He must have been seven years old at the time. With us living in Tennessee we grew away from the traditions of our people," said Nakiya's mother.

"Mother, I don't understand why great grandfather would hold me to that promise. My heart does not long for Dark Antelope, and at the same time I don't want to go against great grandfather's wishes. I don't know what to do."

"Nakiya maybe you can put off giving Dark Antelope an answer until January when Mother and Father come back from Hawaii," suggested Running Wolf. "I know you have your heart set on going to medical school. That knowledge can be as important as being a shaman for our people."

"Excuse me," Blue Heron said pulling back the teepee flap. "I bring a message to Nakiya from Dark Antelope."

"Please come in Blue Heron," said Nakiya's father. "What is the message you are to deliver to my daughter?" He asked motioning to Blue Heron to sit.

"Thank you, but I will deliver the message and then I must leave. The council will make its decision in the morning. Dark Antelope request that Nakiya meet him in the log house of one who has gone beyond. One of you may accompany her to the cabin, but he will speak to her alone."

"Alone?" Nakiya's father asked.

"He has promised me that no harm will come to her and with you outside the door I saw no harm. But that is still your decision to let her go," Blue Heron said addressing her father.

"No don't let…" Spirit Walker started to say before Crow stopped him.

"If you wish to hear, be still," Crow stated.

"It's alright Father. I know you will be outside the door. I will go listen to what Dark Antelope has to say," Nakiya spoke quietly and walked toward the door taking her father's hand they stepped outside the teepee.

Dark Antelope stood looking out the window when Nakiya entered the cabin. His long hair was pulled back and to the side away from his bandaged neck. He wore only fringed leather pants. The amulet that he usually wore around his neck was wrapped around a well developed bicep. When he turned to look at Nakiya she saw a mixture of emotions in his dark eyes.

"What I have to say to you is for your ears only. Do you promise this?" he asked taking a few steps toward her.

Nakiya knew what was coming as she had known Dark Antelope all her life. There would be consequence either way.

"I agree," she responded.

"You were promised to me when you were a baby and I was seven. I lived for the summers when you would stay with grandfather; and every summer I fell more in love with you. I watched you grow into a beautiful women but I also saw you fall away from our traditions. I will not allow that any longer."

Nakiya tightened her fist holding in the anger as she continued to listen to Dark Antelope.

"I know your grandfather wished you and Running Wolf to follow in his footsteps and that he gave the sacred arrows to Running Wolf before the council approved that he would be the next successor. That ruling can still be overturned. Do not look away far me when I'm speaking to you, Nakiya," Dark Antelope fumed walking around her and then came to stand only a few feet away in front of her.

Nakiya still held her tongue though her mind was lashing out at him for even considering taking her freedom away.

"Nakiya you will marry me on January 22. That will be your nineteenth birthday."

"I do not love you, Dark Antelope. Would you wish to be in a loveless marriage?"

"I have enough love for both of us and in time you will come to have feelings for me."

"And if I refuse?"

"You will not be a shaman of our tribe nor will Running Wolf. I will cast a no vote."

"Why would you do that to Running Wolf? He has never hurt you or spoke against you," she spat. Anger danced in her eyes.

"There are worst things that can happen to Running Wolf than being denied to follow in his great grandfathers footsteps," Dark Antelope pledged placing his hands on Nakiya's arms.

"I thought you were honorable Dark Antelope. You do not belong on the elder's council. I will speak to Blue Heron."

"I don't think so Nakiya," he said increasing the pressure slightly on her arms. "Spirit Walker will hunt the demon Shawgun when the snow clings to the mountains."

"I don't believe you. He is not the one."

"He is the one and you know that in your heart. Why would your grandfather allow him to perform the Sundance? He is the one the legend speaks of and he will die."

"No!"

"What would you give to guarantee he and Running Wolf survives?" he asks as the corners of his mouth turn up.

"Anything, Dark Antelope, anything," she said tears filling her eyes.

Kerry woke with a start, sat up in his bed and pulled the covers back.

"Crow are you close?" Kerry asked racing over to the window and raising it up. "Night Eagle, are you out there? Please, one of you answer me please."

"*I am here*," responded Night Eagle. "*You should be sleeping, Spirit Walker.*

"*Night Eagle, is it true that Nakiya will marry Dark Antelope? Please tell me I was just dreaming.*"

"*Dreams can give us great insight, knowledge and inspiration. The future can be changed because it's always in motion. You must let go of Nakiya and stay focused on your quest for the third gift. The more energy you use thinking of Nakiya the less energy Moon Dancer has in reserve to help you, and you will need him. Running Wolf*

185

and Otter may assist you in finding Shawgun, however they will not have the power to help you destroy him."

"Why not?" I asked my heart breaking in two.

"Have faith Spirit Walker. Sometimes we have to let go of the things we love for the better good of all. Now go back to sleep," Night Eagle coached.

Chapter ELEVEN

We'd been at the school for a month and a half now. I was getting efficient in shape-shifting as I was going out every night to practice. I'd talked to Josh and he told me that Nakiya was working slowly on her wedding dress. Her parents were in despair because Dark Antelope wouldn't relinquish his claim so they took Nakiya back to Tennessee. Josh said he would be graduating from Veterinarian school the fifteenth of December so he'd went back with them.

However he promised they were both coming to the ranch for Christmas as they had refused to let their parents cancel their Hawaii trip.

I'd managed to get some great night shots of the nocturnal animals, besides keep Roger in an agitated state. It had been tricky to lose my shadow but between Harley and me we'd managed so far.

I'd shifted into a red tail hawk and was sitting on the rain gutter outside the back door. I could hear the conversation between Roger and Harley.

"Let's go get Kerry and we can work on our models," Roger urged.

"I think Kerry has already gone to bed," replied Harley.

"He's already gone to bed? Right! For someone who goes to bed so early why does he always look like he hasn't slept when he comes to class? I haven't seen him take any photos so he can't say he spends his time in the darkroom." Roger grumbled.

"I'll go in with you if you want to work on your bird. I have a couple of things I could work on," volunteered Harley.

"Naw, forget it," Roger mumbled.

"Why don't you ask him tomorrow if you want to do something, Roger? But tonight I would leave it alone. I also have some things I need to get done tonight in my room," Harley said and started to walk away.

"This place is as isolated as the ranch. I'm going to go fix me a sandwich," Roger snarled.

I saw that Harley didn't respond to Roger's snide remark and continued to his room going inside he shut the door behind him.

Roger fixed himself a sandwich and got a coke out of the fridge after he put everything away. The kitchen clock read 8:15. He took his snack and went outside but after standing on the concrete patio the cold breeze sent him back inside.

The bird shape-shifted and Kerry landed lightly on his feet outside his own partially open window. He couldn't decide if Roger was angry in general or just lonely.

However, he would get more sleep tonight. Roger was right about one thing, he wasn't getting enough sleep. He was still struggling with his first bird and they were scheduled to start another one in six days. Kerry had put all his energy into his shape-shifting and he knew it was time to focus on his taxidermy. It had been easier having his spirit animals guide him outside the school, but inside with John's help he wasn't catching on as quickly as the other guys. It should have been easy with his gift. Wasn't his gift to give the look of life to the animals that were brought to him to taxidermy?

"Oh Moon Dancer please wake up. I know you are weak, is there not a way to help strengthen your soul. I know I'm missing something. Maybe using this gift to shape-shift I've lost the ability to use it as a taxidermist." Kerry sighed.

He closed his window and noticed the envelope that someone had slid under his door. Picking it the letter up he went back over to his bed and sat down before opening it.

"Dear son, I hope this finds you well. I haven't received any newsy letters so I've told myself you're so busy you haven't had time to write home. We are busier than usually in fact Dad had to hire another guide. It seems that word got out about a rouge bear, though there hasn't been another loss since you left.

Josh came and stayed two days before he went back to Tennessee to finish school. He and Jace have become good friends. Danene took him on a trail ride up to the summit.

Jace wanted me to ask you if everything is alright and that he was only a phone call away.

We were sorry to hear about Nakiya's engagement. I know you had feelings for the young woman; however I was so excited to hear that both of them are still coming for Christmas. They're both such fine young people.

Son, if you need anything please call me. I'm counting the days until you return home.

Miss you and love you, Mom."

"*Oh Mom if you only knew*," he thought folding the letter and slipping it back into its envelope. He hadn't realized how much he missed home until he read it. Things have certainly changed in my life and carefree days; will I ever see care free days again?

Sometimes the weight on his shoulders seemed more than he could bear and there were days he would have given up if it weren't for his spirit animals to encourage him. How he missed Shadow, his constant companion when he was home.

It had been weeks since he had heard from Moon Dancer and he only knew he was still there was he felt him inside the corner of his mind.

"Good morning Roger," I said when he came into the kitchen. I was enjoying biscuits and gravy.

"Why do you always have to hang out with that Indian?" he asked scornfully.

I almost choked on the biscuit I was swallowing.

"If you are referring to Harley, it's because he's my friend," I submitted and continued eating.

"Don't you know you should stick to your own kind?" He growled.

"And what kind is that Roger?" I asked.

"White folk of course," he answered taking down a bowl from the cupboard.

"I wasn't brought up that way to distinguish people by the color of their skin, Roger."

"Well you should of. My Pa says people should stay with their own kind."

"I'm sorry to hear that. My Dad says you should judge people by their character and I have found that to be a pretty darn good guide." I said watching Harley walk through the swinging doors. "Morning Harley saved you same biscuits and gravy."

"Thank you Kerry," Harley said as Roger put his bowl back up in the cupboard. "Do you want some Roger I'm sure there is enough for both of us."

"No. I just lost my appetite," and he left the kitchen.

"What was that all about?" Harley asked sitting up to the counter.

"Don't worry about it. It's something that neither one of us can fix. Did you work on your bird last night?"

"I was going to but decided to write my folks instead." He filled his plate. "Do you want coffee or milk?"

"Milk please. I don't know why I'm struggling with my bird Harley."

"I think you should focus all your energy on your taxidermy. It seems you have your other talent down. Did you capture the red tail hawk last night I saw sitting on the eve by the patio before I went to my room?" he smiled at me letting me know he knew it was me.

"No I must have missed him," smiling back as the secret passed between us.

"I believe class that most of you are ready to put on the finishing touches to your birds. The paints are in the supply room and Mr. Chavez can help you with those," John said looking around the room at our projects. He stopped and looked at mine and shook his head slightly. "Kerry I'll help you after I get the others started," he said and smiled.

I looked at my bird with his uneven wings and the cape that seemed just a little small for the form I was using. One wing was spread beautifully and the other looked like it was deformed.

I'd never had such a hard time learning to do something. But since I'd found the cave my whole world had been turned upside down. I felt bad for the bird that I was 'mutilating' or seem to be.

"Alright Kerry, let's take a look at your bird and see what corrections we need to make," John said lifting up the half assembled bird. "I think we can salvage this one so here's what we are going to do. I want you to very carefully take out the wiring on the right wing and cut the threads on the belly and get a smaller form. I'm going to do one along side of you and we'll do it step by step together."

"Thanks John."

"I want you to clear your head of anything else that's distracting you and only concentrate on what's in front of you. Can you do that?" He asked. "I'll be right back."

"You're the teacher's pet now, too huh," Roger said smugly. "You're not so hot after all," he said in passing.

I tried to think what I'd done to Roger, for him to have such a changed attitude toward me. Harley looked at me and shrugged his shoulders.

"Ok Kerry let's get started," John said, setting his materials down next to mine along with a smaller form for me to use.

I disassembled my bird and started over watching John carefully each step he did I followed. What had taken me four and half weeks John and I did in ten hours with the exception of the painting. We were alone in the class room as the others had left hours ago.

"Kerry have you heard from Nakiya," he asked continuing to work.

"No sir. The last time I talked to her was when she heard her grandfather was sick. My mother told me she has gone back to Tennessee."

"Just as well, I guess," he said and dropped the subject.

It was eleven o'clock when I entered my room and saw the tin foil covered dish setting on my desk. I knew it must have been Harley who had left me supper and I was thankful as I was starving. I uncovered the plate that held potato salad, a roast beef sandwich and a bag of chips. I quietly walked back to the kitchen and without turning on a light picked up a can of coke from the refrigerator.

My fingers were sore from the many times I seemed to have found them with a wire. So before I ate I dabbed them with alcohol to take the soreness out. Picking up my sandwich I think I inhaled it. Not realizing how tired I was I caught myself before my face landed in my potato salad. I hurried with it and had it finished in four mouthfuls and then I went to bed so tired nothing but a blank wall entered my mind.

Friday night Roger followed the guys back in to town leaving me and Harley alone at the school. For November the weather was still mild and we hadn't had our first snow as yet.

"You know when I put the sleeping bags back I saw a tent in the supply room. The temperature hasn't dropped to freezing…"

"Are you saying you'd like to go camping, Harley?"

"It would be nice to get away from here for a couple of days and I really don't want to go into town."

"I think that would be a good idea. I brought winter clothes with me in case I heard of a place to do some photo shots. Where did you have in mind?" I asked taking out my heavier coat from the closet and my insulated boots.

"I have another place I'd like to show you up by Simpson. We can do some fishing on the Milk River," Harley said and smiled as he walked out of Kerry's room with Kerry behind him.

"I haven't had any fresh trout since I came here. That sounds so good. I bet we could borrow fishing poles from John."

"Don't worry, I always carry a couple of fishing poles behind my seat in the truck," Harley said opening the door to the supply room. They pulled out the sleeping bags they had used and then the tent.

"I saw a ranch that sells straw. A couple of bales will keep us warm and cushion the ground."

They rounded the corner going back to Kerry's room since it was the larger of the two and saw Roger standing in the hall.

"Where are you guys going with that gear?" he asked not moving from where he stood.

"We are going camping and John gave us permission to use this gear," Harley said continuing down the hall. Would you like to go? There is another sleeping bag in there."

"Yaw I would," Roger declared going back for the other sleeping bag.

Kerry's mouth dropped open when he heard Roger's reply, especially after the conversation they had in the kitchen this week. Since he hadn't told Harley everything that was said, Harley was blind to that side of Roger. It was too late to say anything right now; however he would keep an eye on Roger.

At six o'clock Kerry and Harley had everything packed in the back of Harley's pickup. Kerry knocked on Roger's door and heard him grumble he'd be out in a few minutes.

"I'm going to go lock my door did you lock yours," Kerry asked Harley as they walked back down the hall.

"I did. I'll meet you in the kitchen. Sounds like Roger will be a bit so I'm going to get something to eat."

"I'll be right there. My stomach is rumbling already this morning."

Roger came out of his room with a suit case in his hand and his pillow. Kerry had already put Roger's sleeping bag in the truck. It took all his control not to laugh.

"Roger we'll be back tomorrow. You sure you need all that?" Kerry asked wondering what kind of outfitters Roger came from, because he didn't act the part of having been raised on an outfitters ranch.

Roger just glared at him and took his stuff to the truck, but instead of putting it in Harleys he put it in his own truck bed. Kerry continued to the kitchen thinking how odd this all seemed. Oh well, Harley invited him, maybe he knows or senses something I don't.

"What did you cook Harley that smells so good?" Kerry asked sitting up to the counter.

"Just some hotcakes I added some pineapple to. It will be a few minutes before the bacon is ready."

"Roger put his stuff in his own truck. I guess he plans to follow us."

"Yes that's what I plan to do," Roger said coming into the kitchen. "Did you make enough for me?" He asked looking at Harley.

"Of course I did Roger. Why would you think I'd fix us something and not you? Grab a plate and sit down. Kerry, would you get the milk out of the refrigerator?" Harley asked using the spatula to scoop up two hotcakes and then sliding them on to Roger's plate and then two each on his and Kerry's plates.

Kerry set the milk on the counter and went back over to turn the bacon over. Spreading a generous amount of butter over his hotcakes Roger passed it over to Harley.

"How much butter do you want on these Kerry?" Harley asked.

"The same as you put on yours," Kerry replied knowing the butter would be dripping on to his plate. They had ate enough times together that he knew what Harley liked and how he liked it.

It was eight thirty by the time everything was cleaned up and they were on the road. Roger still determined to drive his own truck followed them. They stopped at the rancher's to buy straw which Roger said he wouldn't need as he would be sleeping in his truck. They also stopped in Havre for a few supplies and goodies.

"It's hard to believe that Roger grew up on an outfitters," Kerry finally said something to Harley.

"We have a saying; never judge a man until you have walked a mile in his moccasins."

"Well, I've heard keep your friends close and your enemies closer." They both started laughing. "But then there are some enemies I don't want anywhere near me," Kerry said soberly thinking of Shawgun and embraced the bear claw he wore around his neck that was his only protection against the demon.

Turning off highway 232 they drove a couple of miles up another dirt road before Harley stopped near a rocky outcrop. There were fewer trees but sagebrush was plentiful. They cleared a flat spot to set the tent up and then scattered the straw inside before placing their sleeping bags inside. They noticed that Roger had wondered off sometime while they were working and neither one of them knew which direction he'd gone.

Kerry took out the firewood they had bought in Havre and placed it by the fire-pit. Taking out a snickers bar from his backpack he tossed one to Harley.

"Where do you think he went?" Harley asked climbing up on the outcrop. "I can't see him anywhere. I guess if he's not back by sundown we'll have to go looking for him. But until then let's get the fishing poles out and go back down the road to the reservoir. Hopefully we can catch supper."

"I'll leave him a note and he can join us if he wants to." I took out a paper and pencil and quickly wrote where we would be and placed it by the fireplace with a small rock on top to stop it from blowing away. "That should do it Harley, let's go," I said putting my pad and pencil back in my backpack.

Settled in on the rocky bank of the Fresno Reservoir we cast our lines out over the crystalline blue water. The reservoir was laid out like an oblong bowl some sides steeper than others making the water inaccessible. I heard there were some area canyons you could consider a miniature Grand Canyon north of the reservoir. There was large rock crevices you'd have a hard time climbing out if you fell in. The rolling hills grew in size considerably the closer you got to the Canadian border. Grasses were plentiful and trees of western Montana were nonexistent.

"Do you have many rattlesnakes around here?" I asked looking at how dry the ground was.

"Yep. And the further east you go the more plentiful they are. But you know they'll warn you if you get too close to them. They don't want to encounter you anymore than you do them besides this time of year they go into their dens."

"I've only seen one or two on the ranch growing up."

"That's because they like it dry and hot," Harley remarked.

"Oh, I've caught one," I yelled standing up to reel him in. "Wow, this thing is big. I thought trout like to fight. I hope he doesn't break the line, I'd hate to lose him."

"It's a walleye I believe. The line will hold. Walleye, they are great eating, Kerry." Harley said smiling.

Reeling the fish closer to shore Harley put the net in the water but missed the first time getting it completely under the fish. My line slacked and I thought he got away. Reeling in my line quickly I found he was still hooked and fought harder with the taunt line.

"Get under him Harley," I laughed watching him.

"Two more like this and we'll have supper."

Roger was sitting next to the fire when we pulled into camp. By the look on his face what had been eating at him he must have walked it off as he seemed more relaxed.

"Have any luck?" He asked when we stepped out of the truck.

"Oh yah. Look at these," I beamed and pulled the three walleye out of the truck bed. "We have enough for supper. You do like fish, don't ya?"

"You bet I do. Fished a lot at home, mostly trout and bass," Roger said stirring the coals around in the fire-pit.

I was glad that Roger had mellowed out. He had a funny sense of humor. We laughed and told stories most the evening.

"I don't know about you guys, but I'm tired," I said standing up from one of the log stumps we had brought with us to sit on. It was too cold to sit on the ground or a rock this time of year.

"That's right you're an early to bed kind of guy. You must have a hell of a lot of nightmares to make you look like you haven't slept all night," Roger grinned but the merriment didn't reach his eyes.

I just looked at him wondering what he was talking about, and then I realized where he wanted to go with that comment. But I wasn't going to take the bait.

"Never mind Kerry, go ahead and turn in. I'm going to sit out here a while longer.

"Don't you get tired of being his gofer, Injun?" Roger asked looking into the fire.

As I took off my boots I listened to Roger and Harley's conversation.

"I don't consider my friendship with Kerry as being his gofer," Harley said.

What was it with Roger? One minute he seemed like a nice guy and the next he was someone different personality wise. I thought.

"Forget it Injun, I'm going to bed," Roger growled and walked over and got inside his truck.

I could hear Harley poking the ambers and I bet he was wishing one of them was Roger. He now wished that Harley hadn't invited the boy from Utah, as it seemed Roger liked to cause contention. Maybe he'd wake up in a better mood in the morning.

Harley played with the ambers until they had all gone out I assumed before I heard him lock his truck up and make his way to the tent.

******

It was early morning when Harley heard someone outside the tent. He pulled his boots back on and his coat before he unzipped the tent and crawled out. He saw something move over by his truck, so he picked up a piece of wood and walked around to the back of his pickup.

He saw stars and went down on his knees as he was hit again across the back.

"I was hoping it was you Injun that woke up first," Roger said pulling Harley's arms back and tying his hands. He also took off Harley's neckerchief and tied it around his mouth. Taking the unconience out body by the arms Roger drug him over to his truck and hoisted him up into the back and then tied his ankles. Pushing Harley toward the cab he then covered him with a canvas.

"Sleep tight, I have work to do," Roger chuckled quietly. Picking up the piece of wood Harley had carried, he threw the log into the fire-pit along with more kindling and soon had blue and red flames. He picked up the coffee pot that Kerry had prepared the night before and set it to heat.

Half hour later he heard Kerry stirring inside the tent. A few minutes later he crawled out carrying his coat which he quickly put on and blew on his hands.

"Little chilly this morning, isn't it," Kerry said walking over to the fire. "Where's Harley?"

"He took off that way and said after you had your cup of coffee to follow him. Said he had something he wanted to show you."

"I will take that cup of coffee."

Roger poured the coffee and one for him and sat back down on the log.

"Sorry about last night. I just haven't been able to spend much time with you and I thought we would have a lot in common living on outfitters and all. My brothers are all quite a bit older than I am and we don't have a lot of comradery. I get the job no one else wants and that leaves me by myself most the time," Roger cited.

"Don't worry about it. Finish your coffee and we'll go find Harley. I'm sure he left us a trail," I said zipping up my coat and then grabbing my backpack out of the tent.

"You won't need that will you?" Roger asked setting his cup down on his stool.

"I don't go anywhere without my backpack. You ready?"

"Oh ya, I'm ready. You can lead; you probably know what signs he would have left for you."

Chapter TWELVE

"Are you sure he went this way? I haven't seen anything giving that indication," I said looking for signs fresh from this morning. "Harley!" I yelled hoping he could hear me.

"Over there I thought I saw something," Roger said urging me in that direction.

"Harley," I yelled again coming upon rocky ground that surrounded a open hole about six feet across.

"That's far enough, Kerry," Roger said curtly.

I turned around and saw the knife in his hand, and fear shuttled down my spine.

"What's going on Roger? Where is Harley and what's with the knife?" I asked not taking my eyes from his.

"Your Injun friend is taking a little nap back at camp, hopefully for a long, long time. I wasn't sure if I would be able to get you out this far before you caught on that you were following my trail from yesterday," he said moving the knife back and forth in front of him. "Down in that hole is a nice nest of rattlers and you're going to be joining them. But first I want what's around your neck."

"I don't have anything around my neck," I said inching away from the whole.

"Don't give me that crap. I know for a fact you have a bear claw and I want it," he said stepping closer to me.

"If I did have one, why would you want it?" Stalling for time I took another step away from the edge. Roger was getting more erratic swinging his knife back-n- forth.

"Someone's willing to give me ten thousand dollars for that claw; now hand it over. I don't want to have to use this knife when the snakes will do a better job. Now give me that claw!"

I grabbed for his arm with the knife and the front of his jacket with my other hand but instead of us falling back away from the cavity we twisted slipping on the loose rock.

"No!" I heard Roger scream as we both went over the edge. I fell on top of him and the knife was knocked out of his hand when we landed. The crisp sound of breakage had to be his back with my weight added to his. I gasped for air as the fall knocked the wind out of me.

I heard the rattles and saw the first strike that hit Roger's face. I rolled off of him onto my backpack and sat up. My breath caught when I moved and was sure I had broken a couple of ribs. The only real stream of light was coming down the center of the opening leaving the bottom in shadows. I tried to reach out with my mind to the slithering reptiles but that sent a sharp pain through my head and my vision blurred.

Not knowing how many snakes were in this pit I had already seen one to many. I was afraid to take in a breath, afraid to move another inch but I still wanted my back against the rock wall. It was only a couple of inches away. I pressed my heel into the dirt and pushed slowly. Hearing the rattles I stopped but felt the first strike as the snake hit my boot. My coat and boots would give me some protection, but my legs were only covered by my jeans and long johns. Fangs could easily pass through them.

I heard Roger groan however I knew it was only a matter of time before he would be dead. A faint voice penetrated my awareness.

"Spirit Walker what danger are we in now?" asked moon Dancer. *"You are holding your breath again,"* he said a little stronger.

"We are in a snake pit."

"What are we doing in a snake pit?" asked Moon Dancer. *"That was not on our agenda."*

"We are in a snake pit with a person that will soon be dead. I don't know what to do, Moon Dancer." Feeling the movement crawl up my arm I tried not to shutter as it continued around my neck. *"I have a snake that has wrapped itself around my shoulders and is moving down the front of me,"* I said shakily sweat beading on my forehead. *"Oh no I feel one wrapping its self around my legs. We're going to die. I'm so sorry Moon Dancer. I failed you."* My tears run down my cheeks.

The fangs passed through my jeans into my thigh and another strike entered at the bass of my throat. I lay back against the rock wall; I could see the faces of my family, Nakiya. *How could I have failed all of them?*

I closed my eyes and I could follow the serum running through my veins. I watched it pass through my arteries into my heart and out the other side. My stomach cramped and I lost my vision as everything around me went black. How many times would I be led into a black abyss, but it was peaceful now. Leaving my body Moon Dancer and I sat on the over side watching my form in the flesh. My face contorted and then I lay silent.

"Spirit Walker this was not the time when I planned to introduce myself. But as many things in your life have been in a hurry I suppose this will have to do. I am one of your Spirit guides," said Snake as he coiled in front of us. *"Very few are chosen to have snake medicine. You are going through initiation as you have seen my venom race through your veins and arteries. You will transmute all poison; be they spiritual, mental or physical. Snake medicine is the power of creation as it embodies psychic energy, alchemy and ascension,"* Snake instructed his tongue flicking in and out as he was eye level with us.

"What is ascension?" I asked glancing over at my still body.

"Ascension is immortality. Snake medicine is the energy of wholeness, cosmic consciousness, and the ability to experience anything willingly, without resistance. With this knowledge you will know all things are equal in creation. Things you experience as poison can be eaten,

ingested, transmuted and integrated if one is in the right state of mind. This medicine will teach you on a personal level that you are a universal being. You can bring about transmutation of fire medicine. Fire energy on the physical plane creates passion, desire and physical vitality. On the emotional plane becomes ambition, creation and dreams. On the mental plane charisma, leadership and on the spiritual plane it becomes wisdom, understanding and connection to the Great Spirit," Snake instructed and then turned to look at my body that appeared pale and lifeless.

"Will this medicine also help Moon Dancer? He has grown weak and I worry about him," I paused and looked at the body of Roger. "How will I explain this?" Then I looked at myself lying in death hoping what Snake was saying was true.

"When you both re-enter your body both of you will feel a surge of energy. Moon Dancer, this should stay with you until you complete your quest if neither of you waste it on other concerns. The demon is reaching out to desperate souls, making them do his bidding. You are going to have to rely on your gut feelings about animal or human alike. Your other spirit animals will also help guide you," said Snake.

"They must have gone on vacation because they didn't warn me about Roger…and Harley. I don't know what Roger has done to Harley!" I exclaimed.

"*Spirit Walker you don't need to yell, we are both right here,*" cited Moon Dancer.

"*There is nothing we can do for the human that sought you bodily harm. Shawgun was given passage into his mind through his greed.*"

"Kerry. Kerry where are you?"

"I'm here. Down here," I mind-spoke.

"*Harley Otter cannot hear you. However he will find you and go for help. Your body is going through transformation as the poison travels throughout your body taking on the power of snake medicine.*" Snake stated.

"I won't turn into a snake or anything like that, no offence," I said quietly.

Snake laughed. "*No you are only receiving snake medicine. By the time Harley Otter returns it will have finished the transmutation of the life-death-rebirth cycle. You will not remember any of what has happened after you*

216

fell until I come to you, and then you will recognize me and we shall speak."

"Kerry, oh Great Spirit please let him be alive," Harley said looking down into the rock cavity. "Kerry can you hear me. Kerry if you can hear me, I'm going for help." He turned and left on the run as I felt the vibration in the earth.

******

How could I have let a white man take me down? Harley thought going over in his mind what had happened and feeling the goose bump on the back of his head. He turned on to the highway and gunned it, not caring about the speed limit. He wouldn't be that lucky to have a cop patrolling the road.

He was just glad that Roger hadn't felt for any weapons. If his knife hadn't been in his boot he'd still be tied up in the back of Roger's pickup. Thinking of the two bodies lying at the bottom of the rock cavity he couldn't tell if either of them was still alive. He was sure he'd seen something slither away from Kerry's body when he'd looked down into the hole.

Ahead he saw a fish and game truck pull out of the park. He laid on the horn and sped up trying to get the ranger's attention. An eighth of mile the ranger pulled over to the side. Harley pulled up behind letting dust fly when coming to a stop and quickly jumped down from his pickup.

"I need your help! I need your help, now!" Harley shouted running up to the ranger.

"Calm down son. Take a breath and then tell me what the matter is," the ranger said putting his hand on Harley's shoulder.

"I have two friends who have fallen into a snake pit, I think. Neither one of them were moving when I found them and I couldn't get down to check'em."

"Okay. Let me call for back up. I'll follow you to where you found them." The ranger said watching Harley pace back and forth like an ant that had lost his direction.

"This is Clark Webster, come back."

"Go ahead Clark," Harley heard crackle through the CB.

"I'm out at the Fresno campground and I have a young man here who says two of his friends may have fallen into a snake pit. He said they weren't moving when he left to get help. We're going back out there now. I'll radio you where we turn off."

"Roger. I'll send back up right away over and out."

"Okay, young man let's go."

Harley jumped back in his truck and squealed a u-turn. It seemed like forever till they reached the turn off point and Harley didn't slow down on the dirt road until he arrived at camp.

At this point they were unable to drive to the location where the boys were laying unconscious (Harley hoped) and he wasn't sure if the ranger knew another way to get closer with a vehicle.

"I had to track them from camp and it's about a quarter mile," Harley said starting up the path.

"Hold on just a minute, young fellow. I need to get my first aid kit and my walkie-talkie so when help gets close, they'll know how to get to us," Ranger Clark stated. Opening up the side of his truck he pulled out a backpack checking to see if everything was there he needed and threw it over his shoulder. "Lead the way; I'll be right behind you. If you're headed where I think you're headed there are a couple of snake pits out that way."

Neither of them spoke as Harley and the ranger jogged the distance to the rock cavity the boys had fallen in. When they reached the rim the ranger set his backpack down.

"Were you able to see any snakes down there when you found them or were they able to tell you?" the ranger asked looking down into the semi-dark hole, seeing portions of the boy's bodies.

"I thought I saw one slither to the side however I can't be sure. I tried to get Kerry to answer me but neither he nor Roger responded."

They could hear the sirens getting closer but Harley didn't want to wait. He had to get to Kerry.

"Tie the rope around my waist and I'll go down and have a look," Harley said looking at the rope the ranger retrieved from the back pack.

"Maybe we should wait till the medic's and the sheriff get here. I don't want you getting snake bit, too."

"I'm not waiting. You can hold the rope or I'm tying it around that buck brush. Either way I'm going down," Harley said adamantly.

"Okay. Take this extender rod in case you see any down there, at least you'll be able to keep them away from you. Don't move the boys in case they have a neck or back injury. You could make their injuries worse if you do. First thing see if they're breathing."

Tying the rope around his waist, Harley started down the hole a flash light tucked inside his jacket and the snake rod around his wrist.

"Kerry…Kerry can you hear me?" called Harley inching his way down slowly watching for any movement that wasn't the boys. Balanced on a small ledge he took out the flash light and shown it around the boys and then around the perimeter of the cavity. Nothing moved. He did see several holes if there had been snakes they could have exited underground. Harley quickened his pace to the bottom. Standing on the ground between the boys he lit the area up again but still seen nothing move. Kneeling beside

Kerry he put two fingers to Kerry's neck and immediately felt a pulse.

"Kerry is still alive," Harley said moving over to Roger. He just had to look at his face to tell he was dead but checked his pulse anyway. "Roger is dead."

"What we got Clark?" Harley heard someone ask the ranger.

"Two young men, one is dead the other still alive. We don't know at this point if they've been snake bit or not."

Flashing his light around again Harley saw a knife under a small soffit. Moving out of the light funnel he stooped over and picked the knife up, putting it inside his other boot.

"Kerry," Harley whispered.

"I'm coming down," yelled the medic. "Did you see any snakes?"

"I thought I did earlier but nothing has slithered since I've been down here," Harley replied.

The medic looked at Roger first. Your right, this young man is dead. Let's get this rope around him and they can pull him up. That will give us more room to work, what did you say his name was?"

"Kerry. Kerry McDaniels," Harley stated.

"Really, Kerry McDaniels the photographer they've been talking about in town?"

"One and the same."

"He sure got himself in a fix down here. Clark lowered the stretcher down. While they're getting that ready I want to check him for snake bites. Looks like the snakes went underground. Shine your light over on his legs. Looks like one bit him on his thigh right here; see the punctures through his jeans." Pulling Kerry's jacket zipper down the medic also looked around his face and neck. "Look another puncture wound at the base of his throat. That's strange the wound is almost completely healed. Has he been bitten before that you know of?"

Harley hadn't dealt with snake bites. But he knew the poison had to come out from the books he had read.

"Not as long as I've known him and that's been only a couple of months."

"Hold the light right here so I can see to cut his jeans," said the medic taking out a pair of scissors from his bag.

He cut Kerry's pants across his thigh enabling to pull the jeans apart to look at the snake bite. "I don't know how to explain it; this bite is almost completely healed, also. I've never seen anything the likes of it."

"Watch your head, here comes the stretcher," Harley said taking hold of the bottom bar and moving it to the other side of the medic. Harley watched as the medic felt for broken bones and put a collar round Kerry's neck.

"I'm going to roll him to his side. Can you put the stretcher under him?"

"I think so," Harley nodded maneuvering the stretcher horizontal behind Kerry.

"Roger. How is Roger?" I whispered.

"Don't worry about Roger right now, Kerry. Try and relax and we're going to get you out of here," the medic responded.

"I can get up myself." Trying to sit up my stomach cinched, and I was nauseated.

"Whoa there pardoner, you just relax." The medic said. "Can you fasten these straps? Hurry," the medic insisted. "I think he's in shock and I don't want him moving around. We don't know what damage he did when he fell."

"Harley?" I whispered again.

"Everything's okay. Don't try to talk. We need to get you to the hospital."

"My throat hurts. No I don't need to go to the hospital," I cried out hoarsely.

"Kerry if you don't relax they'll give you a sedative and put you out. Now just relax they're going to pull you up."

"Moon Dancer, are you all right? Talk to me."

"I'm fine Spirit Walker, sleep."

******

Two days later Kerry opened his eyes to a white ceiling, an IV hooked up to his arm, and someone was holding his hand.

"Mom what are you doing here?" I asked looking behind her I saw my dad. "What happened? Where are Harley and Roger?"

"Your friend Roger is dead, Kerry. He broke his back in the fall and was snake bit. He was gone they say before they brought him up out of that hole the two of you fell in. They still can't explain why you're still with us since you had two snake bites. But thank God that you are," his father exclaimed.

"Harley went down to get something to eat. He hasn't left this room. He called us when they brought you in. John is out in the waiting room with Rachael. They said they'd stay until they knew you were out of danger. It was nice meeting them but I'd rather done it under different circumstances," Sally said bending over to kiss him on the forehead. "I'll go let them know you're awake.

"We've been through more bumps and bruises with you than you're other siblings put together. You want to tell me what happened? It seems your friend Roger wasn't from Utah after all, and at this point they don't know where he comes from. He was carrying a fake ID." Dad reported.

"Glad to see you with your eyes open and alert," John said coming into my room with Rachael "Everyone in the class hopes you'll be back soon."

"I don't know about that," Dad said. "I think we'll take him home with us. We've had too many scares with him this year."

"I think Jacob, Kerry should stay here and finish what he's started," Mom replied gently putting her hand over her husband's and the other one on Kerry's shoulder.

"Moms right Dad. Things are just coming together and I'd probably lose that knowledge if I had to wait another year."

"Did you find out anything more about Roger, John?" I asked squeezing my mother's hand lightly.

"I called that outfitters in Utah and they had never heard of Roger. This has never happened before at the school that someone would sign up with a false ID to get into class," John said. "What happened anyway out there?"

"I remember we were going to find Harley. Roger said he'd left earlier and he wanted us to meet him as soon as I woke up that morning. We followed a trail about a quarter of a mile when Roger and I were standing looking down into this big hole in the ground and I slipped on loose rock. I grab his coat to regain my balance and the next thing I knew I was laying on top of him at the bottom of that hole. That's all I remember."

"Kerry you're awake," Harley shouted excitedly setting his tray down on the empty bed next to Kerry's.

"I need to go call Jace. I think he has called every hour since we've been here. I'll be right back," said his father.

"I'll go with you. I need to get them to bring something up here for Kerry to eat now that he's awake," his mother declared following his dad into the hallway."

"Now we know you are alright, Rachael and I are going to leave. We'll see you soon," he said looking at me and then nodding toward Harley.

"You have some pretty cool parents. Your mother brought cookies with her."

"Yaw, I wouldn't trade my parents for anything."

"Kerry the police want to talk to you about what happened?"

"I knew that was coming. Harley, how's your head? Roger told me he hit you over the head with a log. Said you were dead and that he tied you up and put you in the back of his pickup to dispose of you. What are we going to tell the police?"

"The truth is always the best. Did Roger say what he wanted or did he just flip out?"

"He told me that he was going to get paid ten thousand dollars to get the claw that hangs around my neck," I said, my hand going to the leather thong that held the bear claw. Feeling nothing I went into a panic.

"Oh no, it's gone! My Bear claw is gone."

"On second thought maybe not the whole truth, no one would believe us anyway, at least in the white man's world," Harley commented.

Chapter THIRTEEN

"Kerry I didn't see it on you before they took you down to x-ray. Did Roger have it before you both fell down that hole?"

"No. But I felt him clutch my shirt around my neck as we went over the edge. Could my leather string have broken in his grasp? I don't know. Could it be lying at the bottom of the snake pit or could Roger have had it in his hand? I don't know, I don't know! Harley I've…"

"You don't know what?" My mother asked entering the room with a tray which she set on the small table, before she rolled it over to my bed. "What's the matter, you seem agitated."

"Mom I've got to get out of here. I can't stay here and you and Dad need to go back home, I said nervously running my fingers through my hair.

"Kerry," Harley said standing close to the bed now. "I need to leave for a little while and I suggest you relax and visit with your parents."

I realize then what Harley was up to. He was going to go find where they had taken Roger's body and check for my bear claw among his things. I laid back and tried to relax a bit or at least give the impression I was relaxed.

Wonder if Shawgun knew I was without his bear claw. Maybe Shawgun was here in Havre because it wasn't until Roger went into town with the other guys that he started acting strange. Now I've put Harley in danger as well as my parents and...

"Kerry." My dad's voice brought me back to the present. "The sheriff wants to know if you'll answer some questions?" I felt my forehead bead with perspiration and my pulse quickened. *Relax, just relax I have nothing to feel guilty about. Oh Shadow I wish you was here and Moon Dancer...*

"I'm close Kerry."

"Shadow is that really you?" or was Shawgun playing games with me.

"Your mother insisted that I come with them and you know she usually wins a discussion with your dad. I can't come up but perhaps you can come down later. Until then relax, if evil comes I will warn you."

I felt my shoulders loosen. Just knowing Shadow was near made it easier to think.

"Kerry, he's waiting," Dad said nodding toward the door.

"Sorry Dad. Yes I can answer any question he has." I laid back into my pillow and sipped the orange juice out the straw. I smiled as the sheriff walked into my room. He reminded me of Ron, our ranger back home, easy going, always smiling. The sheriff carried his hat and strolled into my room acknowledging my mother first.

"Mrs. McDaniels, Mr. McDaniels, would you mind if I spoke to your son alone for a few minutes?"

Dad started to protest and Mom put her hand on his arm.

"I think we'll go down to the cafeteria and get something to eat," she said guiding my dad toward the door.

"I'll be fine Dad," I said and smiled. With Shadow close, I felt calmer and I had nothing to hide except a demon that was trying to kill me and using innocent people to help him. Well maybe Dark Antelope wasn't so innocent but still.

"Kerry, I'm Sheriff Crawford," he said turning the chair around and then sat down placing his arms on top of the chair back.

"I've heard some different stories about what happened, however I would like to hear from you exactly what got you landed down in that snake pit," he said his eyes moving to the base of my throat where they said I'd been bitten.

My skin was slightly discolored I was told but the puncture wound was now completely healed. That in itself was a phenomenon I'd been told.

"Why don't you tell what you know about Roger Hopkins first," the sheriff said his eyes meeting mine.

He seemed to look beyond my physical body into my soul and I wondered if he could also see Moon Dancer tucked away in the shadows. I knew that was a good indication that if I lied the sheriff would know. I felt uneasy.

"I met Roger a couple of days before school started. He seemed like a likeable guy. Harley used to kid me about having a shadow."

"Why was that?"

"He liked to follow me around and Harley said he'd get upset when I'd go to bed early. I thought he wanted to hang out because we both came from Outfitters and had something in common. I remember he went into town one weekend with the other guys in the class and he seemed different when he returned. I didn't know if he was lonely or depressed. He seemed agitated most the time after that."

"Is that why you invited him to go camping with you?"

"I didn't. Harley asked him. I think Harley felt sorry for Roger even though he called Harley an Injun when the others weren't around," I said fluffing my pillow.

"Kerry answer his question but do not let him touch you," Shadow warned

"Did that bother Harley that Roger called him an Injun?"

"He didn't act like it. I don't think anything gets Harley riled up. I've known him over two months and I've never seen him upset about anything."

"Okay, tell me about the camping trip."

I tried to look relaxed as I continued my story.

"Roger took off on his own while Harley and I went fishing the first day and he seemed in a better mood when we came back to camp," I said pulling the bed table closer to me using it for a barrier.

"Didn't it seem odd that Harley would leave before you woke up?" He asked.

"Not really. I know Harley likes to meditate and would go where no one was around."

"What kind of mood was Roger in when you got up that morning?"

"He seemed in a really good mood and he told me Harley had left and I was to follow after I woke up. Roger pointed out which direction Harley had gone and we started walking. Have you been Havre's sheriff long?" I asked and watched the surprised expression of my question steal across the sheriff's face. Shadow was barking.

The sheriff stood up sliding his hand into his pants pocket and I gripped the table in case I had to use it to keep the sheriff way from me.

"Sorry Sheriff," Mom said rushing into the room. "Kerry I just talked to Jace again and he said I had to bring this to you right now."

In her hand was the bear claw on a new piece of leather. She placed the stringed claw around my neck. I looked at the sheriff and whatever he was holding onto in his pocket he let go of and brought his hand up to his belt hooking his thumb over it.

"Thanks Mom. I thought I'd lost it in the snake pit. Is that Shadow I hear barking," I asked still keeping my eyes on the sheriff.

"Why yes. Your dad went down to see what the ruckus was about. That's so unlike Shadow to bark like that. I wanted to surprise you. Shadow has been such a mope lately," she said going to the window. "Oh Sheriff did you still have questions for Kerry?"

"No Mam. I found out all I need to know. You have a good day now," he said smiling at her as he left my room.

"Alright Kerry, before your dad gets back up here I want to know what's going on!" She said picking up my hand. "I've never heard your brother so insistent."

"Mom you have to trust me until I'm free to tell you what has happened."

"Kerry I feel this dark cloud over you. I've felt your life in danger and if I expressed my feelings to your father he'd insist we take you home as soon as you are released from the hospital."

"Mom, please have faith in me a little longer and when I can, I will tell you everything. I will. But I have to finish this. Just know I'm not alone dealing with this test."

"Strange, that's what your brother told me. The two rattlesnake bites you took should have killed you, I'm told. I know there is a higher power watching over you…

"I can't believe, Shadow," my dad stated entering my room. "He growled at the sheriff when he walked by and I had to hold him back."

"Thanks, Shadow."

******

Several hours later Harley returned. His eyes looked tired when he shuffled into my room and sat down on the extra bed next to the tray he'd brought up earlier in the day. Mom and Dad had left and were going to dinner with John and Rachel.

"I couldn't find it Kerry. When I talked to the attendant at the morgue he told me someone had already come for Roger's clothing."

"It's alright, Harley. Mom had the bear claw and had strung it on a new piece of leather," I said holding it up for him to see.

"Well that's one less worry. I did find something in the back of my truck that was interesting. I believe before Roger knocked me out that he took his suitcase out of his truck and put it in mine thinking he would drive mine away. Anyway I went through it. I found out how he knew about your sister and the rest of the family," he said handing me a folded newspaper.

"I remember this. Danene had talked to a reporter at one of her shows and he did this write up. But Harley that would mean that Roger knew before classes started that I was enrolled."

"You're right. There were two possibilities maybe three who would have known you would be starting class in September and that would be Mr. Chavez, Mr. Monroe and maybe Rachael," Harley surmised. "It's hard to consider any of the three. What would be the motivation for any of them to set you up? John did have you come out two weeks early."

"If it was John, wouldn't he would have had Roger come in early also? I mean, no one would be around if something happened to me. No, I would eliminate John as being the one who contacted Roger. I don't know Chavez nor have I spent any time with him other than in class, how about you?"

"I can't say that I have. I thought I heard him say to one of the other students that in the summer he goes down to Mexico. They were asking about summer classes. Maybe we'll never know, Kerry. Oh, I saw your dog in the back of your dad's pickup. He's beautiful. What do you call him?"

"Shadow."

"*Kerry, you alright?*"

Surprised that I heard him in my head I grinned. It was nice knowing he was close.

"*I'm fine. Mom and Dad alright?*"

"*Yes. They were offered to stay out at the Monroe's', however they will be staying again at the motel.*"

"*Thanks Shadow.*"

"You're speaking to your dog?" Harley asked lifting up the cover of the lunch he'd left earlier and wrinkled up his nose.

"Yes, in fact he warned me about the sheriff that came in to question me. Shadow told me not to let the sheriff touch me. I was nervous when Crawford reached in his pocket and started to pull something out when Mom rushed into the room. She put the claw back around my neck and then the he said he found out everything he wanted to know and left."

"What did Crawford look like, Kerry? I don't remember a sheriff named Crawford."

I didn't get a chance to answer Harley as the nurse come in and told him he'd have to leave now. The doctor was making his evening rounds.

I was in deep thought about my instructors, Monroe and Chavez, when the doctor came in to my room looking over my chart I assumed. I pushed away the bed table from across my lap and lined it parallel with my bed.

"Do you realize just how lucky you are young man?" the doctor said closing the chart. I've never seen anyone get snake bit twice without life-threatening consequences. Most die and all you have are two spots of discoloration. I can't for the life of me explain it. We're going to take one more sample of blood and if that comes back clear of anything suspicious you can go home in the morning," he said listening to my heart and then my lungs.

He moved back my covers and then ran his fingers over the discoloration on my thigh.

"Does that hurt," he asked looking at the strange shape the colors made.

"No sir. My throat is sore and my ribs hurt some from the fall. That's about it," I replied.

He looked at my throat and felt the spot at the base of my neck.

"If I hadn't seen the fang marks myself when they brought you in I wouldn't have believed it when they said you were snake bit. You certainly have some higher power watching over you," he said checking my ribs. "Your ribs are bruised and will be sore for a while. It doesn't look like you ate your lunch would you like me to order you something up?"

"No thank you. I'm fine, Sir." I said looking over at the box of Mom's cookies peeking out from under my extra blanket. I didn't want to tell him I didn't trust anyone fixing me something to eat. Who knows what might find its way into my food.

"The nurse will be in in a few minutes to take your blood. Alright son I'll see you in the morning."

I watched the doctor leave the room and then retrieved the box of cookies Mom had brought up that was still half full. They would fill me up. I laid my head back on my pillow savoring a peanut butter cookie.

"*Kerry,*" Shadow mind-spoke.

"Shadow, where are you?" I asked

"Look out your window," he replied.

I hurriedly pushed back my coverings and stepped onto the floor. I swayed a moment getting my balance but made it to the window. Looking out onto the lawn I saw Shadow. I wanted to hug him; I'd missed him so much.

*"I will stay here and wake you if I feel danger. You need sleep and don't get sick eating all those cookies tonight. "*Shadow said grinning up at me before I saw him lay down in the grass.

Chapter FOURTEEN

I opened the door to my room and let it open wide so Harley, Shadow and my parents could follow me inside.

"Dad, check out the darkroom, it's the second door," I said sitting on my bed. I put my arms around Shadow and rubbed my check against him. I was ecstatic that John said Shadow could stay the remainder of this session.

"This is very nice, Kerry," Mom said sitting down beside me. "After we leave, remember to call Jace at home. You'd better call collect because you probably won't have enough dimes. I know if he hadn't been needed at home he would have been here."

"I will call him Mom. Have you heard from Nakiya or Josh," I asked hoping for a yes.

"Jace has talked to Josh. He told us that Josh would be taking his finals next week and that Nakiya put starting school in January on hold. They both still plan to come for Christmas and that will be nice."

Nakiya's news made my stomach feel like it had been kicked by a mule. There was only one reason Nakiya would put off school and that would be to marry Dark Antelope. That thought tightened the knot growing in my belly. I had to find a way to stop that from happening. I just wasn't sure how I was going to do that.

"You okay, son. You look a little pale," Dad asked leaning against the door jamb of the darkroom.

"I'm just tired is all. That fall took more out of me that I thought. I can still see Roger's eyes looking into mine and when that snake bit him, how fast his face swelled... I could have been the one on the bottom.

"In time Kerry, those fragments will fade," Harley said. "I'm going to go take a shower and get out of these clothes. It was nice to meet you Mr. and Mrs. McDaniels. I hope to see you again."

"You have an open invitation anytime to come to the ranch, Harley," Mom stated standing up and then walking over to my dad.

"I think we need to leave, also. They have predicted snow at the pass and we need to get on the other side before it starts. This winter is supposed to be a bad one, I guess we'll see," Dad said putting his arm around my mother's shoulders.

I stood up and gave them both a hug.

"Thanks for bringing Shadow. I have missed him something terrible."

"I know the feeling has been mutual for Shadow. We've also missed you at home Kerry. The next month won't go by quick enough. Follow the doctor's instruction," Dad said walking with Mom to the door.

After they left I took a chair to the phone in the hall. The call would be lengthy and I wasn't up to standing for very long. Mom had been right I wouldn't have had enough dimes for the phone.

"Jace, Shawgun has been here in Havre. I know that's who got to Roger. But the funny thing is that he knew I was coming here before the class started. Since he didn't come from that outfitter in Utah someone had to give him information about our place, Danene and my photography."

"Where would Roger have received the information? Or better still who would known that information? That article you talked about was from the local newspaper back east where Danene did the show."

"I don't know about the newspaper but my coming to the school that would have been John Monroe and Mr. Chavez and maybe Rachael, John's wife," I said trying to reposition my ribs so it didn't hurt so much to breath.

"Didn't you send your registration to the school before you found the cave?"

"You're right I did. So are you thinking it had to have come from someone at the powwow? Someone who knew I was going to go to school in Havre?"

"Kerry when I talk to Josh next I'll ask him, as we talk at least once a week now. Finish telling me everything that has happened so I can pass it on to him."

"By the way Jace, thank you for telling Mom to get my claw back to me. I don't know what would have happened if she hadn't come in when she did. I think Harley was going to find out who that Crawford guy was. Harley didn't think he was a real sheriff."

"I feel better now that Shadow is there with you. I didn't take much to convince her to take him with them to

Havre. When I talk to Josh again I'll give you a call. It won't be to long till you'll be home."

"Thanks, I feel better having Shadow here. So what's Josh going to do after he graduates?" I asked shifting on the hard chair again.

"He's moving up to Browning. He'll be staying in his Great Grandfather's cabin. His parents are going to bring their nephew out to Tennessee to help them on their ranch. Josh said they had increased the number of horses they were going to train but his parents had told him it was more important for him to take his place as the tribes Shaman," Jace explained.

"And what about Nakiya?" I held my breath but not long enough to wake Moon Dancer.

"She is still coming out for Christmas. Josh said she's been real quiet and the only thing she talks about is coming to the ranch in December."

"I can't believe she agreed to marry Dark Antelope, even though her duty…"

"Kerry you have enough to worry about without putting more baggage on your shoulders."

"I know Jace, but I love that baggage." I finally admitted my feelings for Nakiya.

"Kerry your first love is always the hardest. I'm sure there will be someone else in the future."

"I don't want anyone else. But you are right I need to concentrate on getting that last gift back and taking care of the demon Shawgun. Moon Dancer's strength has subsided and I worry about him," I said, as I recalled how weak his voice had been in the snake pit. "I'm tired and I think I'll turn in.

When I hung up the phone I still had a lot of unanswered question. However, I felt better having gone over every detail with Jace about what had happened here.

I was up and down the next day. I still had a lingering headache and my bruised ribs made it difficult to breath. By Friday all the color was gone from my snake bites. I was eager to get back to class on Monday not only to start on my final project but I wanted to see my class mates. Thinking they would have some information that they didn't think important that they could pass on to me about Roger. I needed to know Roger's contact, not convinced it could have been Chavez or John.

"Shadow when we go to class on Monday hopefully you'll be able to pick up any evil vibes' from Chavez."

"Evil has been in your room at one time as remnants still linger here."

"Dark Antelope has been in here a few times, Shadow."

"The evil has no name. Have you talked to your other spirit animals?"

"Not since I've been able to shape-shift on my own. When all this happened I was thinking they had left me."

"They must feel confident you can handle situations on your own. They are always near if you need them. You have a new spirit animal I've not met, have you not?"

"Yes Shadow, he is Night Eagle. He has taken me spirit walking on more than one occasion. We went to browning when they were gathered around Wolf Talker's last hours, another time when we watched Dark Antelope mix the poison he tried to get me to consume."

"You said you can shift on your own now, tomorrow night we will run. We will find your spirit animals and listen to their guidance. You need to rest. I believe Harley

Otter is on his way to your room with something that will help your ribs and ease your breathing," Shadow said as there was a knock on my door.

"Come in Harley."

"Kerry I have brought you something to ease your breathing and quicken the healing process of your bruised ribs," he said. Both hands were full and he strolled over to the desk and set the contents down.

"Is this like the wrap we used when I was injured by that bear?"

"No. This will lie over your ribs and it has different herbs. And this you will drink. Yes, it will taste horrible."

He answered my question before it crossed my lips. I smiled grateful for the friendship that Harley and I had.

"Harley this is Shadow. Shadow this is Harley Otter my good friend."

Shadow walked up to Harley and gave him his paw.

"Shadow it's good to meet you. I've heard a lot about you."

"Shadow, Otter can mind-speak, if you want to try it with him."

"Thank you, Otter for helping Spirit Walker." I heard him say.

"You're welcome Shadow. Spirit Walker has a great task to accomplish and I'm honored to be able to help him."

"Drink, I want to make sure you drink it all. I know if I leave before it is drunk, you will set it aside."

I put the cup to my mouth and took a small sip. A fire inflamed the membranes in my mouth and scorched down my throat.

'Don't play with it Kerry. Take it all, there is not that much to consume," Harley smiled.

"The fire only lasts a few minutes."

"A few minutes I might not have a mouth left," I sputtered.

"Hurry, the rest," Harley said.

I quickly downed the rest of the liquid and felt the heat clear to my toes. However I was surprised when I took a breath that it wasn't as painful. Wither my mouth and throat turned to ash after being scorched was another thing.

"You'll rest well tonight. I'll see you in the morning. Good night and goodnight Shadow."

I could hear Shadow laughing sitting by my bed.

"You think it's funny Shadow. Next time I'll save you a portion to take." I could hear the echo of Harley's laughter along with Shadow's on the mind-link that connected us.

Rolling over to sit up, my ribs didn't yell at me to stop moving. Why was I surprised when I knew how well Harley's other concoctions had worked for me. My stomach was the only thing complaining this morning as I listened to numerous growls. I noticed that Dad had put a bag of dog food behind the door and Shadow's dishes.

I filled his bowl with food and the other with water setting them out of the way so they wouldn't get knocked over and started laughing.

"What's so funny, did I miss something," Shadow asked rubbing his head against my leg.

"I was thinking why I was worried about knocking over your dishes with just the two of us here. It's not like we were home. Home, that word sounds good. You know Shadow, I'm getting homesick."

I put my camera on the bed checking that I had enough film for the day before leaving my room to go to the kitchen.

"Shadow I'm going to the kitchen so when you're done that's where you'll find me," I stated pushing the door wide so it would stay open. Harley was shuffling down the hall when I walked out of my room. "You hungry," I asked meeting him by the phone.

"You got that right. Mrs. Cantrell brought over fresh blueberries so you could fix your favorite blueberry hotcakes. That's your favorite according to your mom."

"That does sound good. Hopefully she brought bacon, also. Harley I was thinking I'd like to go back out to that snake pit and take pictures. Actually I was thinking of the whole area we were at. Pictures sometimes will pick up things that we miss with our eyes."

"Sure. Everything happened so fast I didn't think to look for anything either, but then again I don't know what

I'd be looking for. The police are saying it was an accident so they only went back out there to bring Roger's truck in to town," Harley said pushing through the swinging doors of the kitchen.

"I wonder if they went through Roger's room? I know he had his suitcase with him when we left to go camping," I commented taking down the blue mixing bowl. "He could have left something behind. I think we should check after we finish eating. By the way what did you find out about Sheriff Crawford?"

"Talked to Hank, the sheriff here in Havre, and he said he didn't know of a sheriff around these parts by the name of Crawford. Said Crawford could be from another county or a sheriff looking for Roger Hawkins."

"Don't you think it would take longer than a couple of days to get the word out about Roger, especially since they considered our fall an accident to bring someone in to talk to me about it."

"Yes it does Kerry. But we know what Crawford looks like so at least if he shows up again that will be to our advantage."

"*I know his scent. He will not be getting close to you without me knowing*," Shadow stated coming into the kitchen. He lay down at the end of the counter.

Pouring the washed berries into the batter I mixed them in lightly. Harley had the bacon cooking and the coffee was perking sending the aroma swirling around our noses. My stomach growled again and my mouth started to salivate.

We were eating when Shadow sat up. Someone was coming down the hall we could hear the click of their boots on the tile floor.

"I'm glad to see you up," John announced coming into the kitchen. "Your class mates were wondering if you'd be back in class on Monday."

"Yes, I'll be back. It seems longer than a week I've been gone. John have they found out who Roger really was?"

"Not that I've heard Kerry. I was told that they took his finger prints but that could take awhile. I can't think for the life of me why someone would give false ID to register for class. But then again he could have been using that name for a long time. People do that. It was the connection to that outfitter in Utah he claimed to have that I wonder about. I've got to go. I stopped in to see if you were alright. I'm taking Rachael up to Browning to see her brother. I'll see you on Monday. Hello Shadow," John said rubbing him behind the ears before he left.

The time it took to get to the place we camped seemed shorter; perhaps it was because I knew where we were going. Harley parked just before our camp site. The police had to park here when Roger and Harley's trucks were parked in the same location. It was large enough for only the two trucks. Picking up my camera I placed the strap around my neck and stepped down from the truck slowly.

"I'll go around this side and look," Harley said going to the north side of the camp.

Shadow and I went around the south side and I started snapping pictures. The fire-pit area hadn't been disturbed. I noticed where Roger had sat waiting for me to wake that morning, that there were marks in the dirt he sketched with a stick. I finished taking pictures at different angles before I called Harley over.

"Do these markings mean anything to you, Harley," I asked as he walked careful around the area.

"They are symbols but the meaning I'd have to ask my father. That's something I've not studied a whole lot. See here where the line ended abruptly; most people would continue on through with the motion. I found this under a peculiar stack of rocks. Does it mean anything?" He asked handing me an arrow head with a lightning mark and two dots etched upon both the front and the back.

I sat down on the stump holding what looked like one of Moon Dancer's arrow heads.

"*Moon Dancer, wake up! I need you to look at something.*"

"*What is it, Spirit Walker,*" he asked stronger than I'd heard him in a long time.

I was surprised he answered me so quickly.

"Is this one of your arrow heads? Harley found it under a peculiar stack of rocks' on the outside of our camp area. I held the rock in my hand so Moon Dancer could examine it through my eyes.

"It looks like one of mine; however I can't recall placing it under a stack of rocks. How were the rocks stacked?"

"Harley can you explain the rock stack so I can explain it to Moon Dancer?" I asked.

"Come over here and I will restack it as I found it."

I followed Harley to the back side of where the tent had been set up. I watched as he meticulously restacked the rocks.

"Kerry these rocks were touched with evil hands the evil I felt in your room at the school," Shadow stated.

I heard Moon Dancer murmur with each rock that Harley position into place. When Harley finished Moon Dancer sighed heavily. I knew whatever he was going to say was not going to be good news.

"Spirit Walker this is a warning against one of my own. With Wolf Talker now on Icebis I believe the attack will be on Josh or Nakiya."

"I haven't told you that Nakiya has said she will marry Dark Antelope. I believe he has threatened her with something for her to give up her ambition to become a doctor."

"Harley, Moon Dancer says this is a warning against Josh or Nakiya. Did I tell you that Moon Dancer in his youth saved his sister Spotted Fawn from Shawgun using her as a blood sacrifice?"

"No you didn't tell me that. That might be Shawgun's intention with Nakiya," Harley said dishearten.

"I know she is safe right now as she is in Tennessee. I guess she is staying there until she comes to Rose Feather for Christmas. I don't blame her I wouldn't want to be around Dark Antelope. I still can't believe that her parents would go along with this knowing how she feels."

"Here is something to think about, Kerry; if Dark Antelope and Nakiya marry and Shawgun's intention is to sacrifice her, Shawgun would need to kidnap Nakiya before the marriage is consummated."

"What does that have to do with it?" I asked puzzled.

"Nakiya has to be a virgin when Shawgun sacrifices her."

"Don't you think that Dark Antelope would know that bit of information?"

"*If a bit of Shawgun's evil resides inside Dark Antelope that small portion of information he could keep shadowed,*" said Moon Dancer.

"Meaning?"

"Meaning, that Dark Antelope is setting up Nakiya for Shawgun's sacrifice; and doesn't even know it."

I felt like I'd been kicked in the stomach again but this time I might lose my breakfast. I sat down before I fell down. Shadow nuzzled against my leg and I put my hand through his black and silver coat hoping that some of his calm would transfer to me as it did on many occasions.

"What is it Kerry," asked Harley.

"Moon Dancer thinks that Dark Antelope is setting up Nakiya for Shawgun's sacrifice and doesn't even know it," I said letting that information sink in. "I think we have everything from here let's walk out to the snake pit. Maybe Shawgun has placed something out there"

"I will have to find a way to kill the demon Shawgun before that happens. I think the wedding ceremony is the later part of January."

We both walked out to the snake pit, both in our own thoughts. I was wondering what miracle was going to happen?

"You mean how are you going to find the stolen gift, save the girl and kill the demon and be home for supper," asked Moon Dancer.

"Doesn't that only happen in fairy tales," I replied, my eyes down cast. *"I'm not in a fairy tale and the weight of this task seems to be getting heavier and heavier."*

"This way Kerry," Harley yelled. "You need to stay alert out here or you may not be as lucky if you fall in another hole."

He was right. I had let myself drift when I should be paying attention. I stood still for a moment and took pictures of the surrounding area. I saw Harley stop and knew he must have found the pit.

"Kerry you can't dwell on anything than what's in front of you." Moon Dancer said adamantly his joking turned serious. *"You drain my energy. And when we find Shawgun I'm going to need all the energy I can muster if we are to defeat him."*

"Sorry. I'll try harder to stay focused." Hearing Shadow bark, I looked up to see Sheriff Crawford coming up out of the snake pit. I didn't know why but I snapped several pictures of him in succession and by the time I

reached Harley he was gone. Shadow was standing over Harley licking his face. I looked in the direction in which Crawford had run and saw nothing. I wasn't going to go after him. When I reached Harley he was sitting up.

"What happened? I asked urgently looking him over for any wounds.

"It wasn't a man; it was a demon, a lesser one than Shawgun but a demon none the less.

I looked over the edge and the demon in Crawford's appearance, floated up from the bottom, his power threw me back."

"Why would a demon be out here, Harley?"

"I'm thinking that he was hoping to find the snake that bit you and to use his venom for a poison."

"Do you think he found it? Do you think he got the venom?"

"I feel Shawgun is getting more aggressive in his search to stop you. He must fear you and Moon Dancer indeed. Take your pictures and let's get back to the school."

Chapter FIFTEEN

I set things up in the dark-room. It had been a while since I had developed film and I was anxious to see these as much as Harley. Harley went to the kitchen to make us something to eat and Shadow followed him while I worked in the dark-room. Shadow had stayed close to him since we got back. I was hoping the demon hadn't left a residue on Harley.

When I heard them return to my room I'd finished one roll of film. I'd wait until after I ate to finish the other roll. Some things had precedence and right now that was my stomach. The smell was enticing and brought me out of the dark-room.

"How is he Shadow?" I asked as Harley set the tray down on the desk.

"I can sense no evil residue on Otter. I believe he is a lucky young man. That demon could have hurt him if he'd taken the time."

"Okay, what are you two talking about," Harley Otter asked popping the cap off two coke bottles.

"You, of course. I was just asking Shadow how you were feeling."

"Other than the spot he punched me with his power I feel alright," he said rubbing the spot on his chest. "I wasn't sure how you like your burgers and dogs so I just cooked them the way I like mine. There was a macaroni salad in the fridge and Mrs. Cantrell said there was a chocolate cake in the cake round."

The sun was setting when we spread the pictures out on the table. The first one was of the markings made in the dirt by the fire-pit.

"I'll send this to my father. It should only take a day or two to reach him," Harley remarked.

"I was astonished at the picture of what I thought was Crawford. The image was distorted and you couldn't make out any distinguishing marks. In the snake pit when I had taken the shot of the snake lying at the bottom in the center, its fangs were missing. Not a good sign."

I was tired when Harley left my room to go to bed.

"What do you think of Harley, Shadow, now you have had time to spend with him?"

"He'll be a good friend to you, Spirit Walker. The light is strong in him," Shadow remarked.

"Yes, Otter has been brought up by his father Blue Heron," said Moon Dancer. *"Blue Heron had the Spirit when he was very young and was gifted with many gifts. Otter is one of those gifts and he has been raised to know the spirit. Otter and Running Wolf, you'll be able to trust your life with. I need to sleep as you do Spirit Walker.*

******

Monday morning when I entered the class room I was swamped with question from my classmates. As far as anyone knew it was an accident when Roger and I fell into the snake pit and the only mystery was why Roger had lied about his name and residence. Everyone was open with the knowledge they had of him. Perhaps we would never know who Roger was and where he came from.

Working on my Red Tail Hawk my fingers moved with ease pulling the cape over the mold and fastening the wings and tail to my bird. I was in awe considering the trouble I'd had doing anything with my bird before the accident with Roger. Even the smallest details I easily did.

"Kerry, you are a surprise. This Red Tail Hawk is looking beautiful. I wondered at one time if I'd be able to give you a certificate in December. Sometimes it takes a while for things to click. Wednesday you should be able to start painting," John said looking at the bird closer.

I wondered what happened because I had the same worry John had just admitted to about getting my certificate. Looking over at Shadow he was enjoying the attention of Garret Ritter the Texan, apparently there was no evil coming from the older cowboy.

"You have a well behaved dog, Kerry. This is the first time John has ever allowed a pet into class," Mr. Chavez admitted. "I bet you have had him since he was a puppy."

"I have, in fact it's the first time we've been separated other than my time at school during the day. Everyone says we are attached at the thigh."

"He's a beautiful dog. Your work is looking much better; maybe his presence has made the difference. Animals contribute many things in our lives."

"Have you had a special animal in your life, Mr. Chavez?"

"I have Kerry." He said and moved on to help Carl.

I slid open my window and Shadow jumped through and I followed. Looking at the beauty of the night sky, the star constellations, and feeling the cold that wrapped itself around everything was part of Montana's beauty. I could smell snow in the air. Tonight could be the first snow fall of the season.

I shape-shifted in my wolf form and loped beside Shadow over the open prairie headed for the ravine where I'd always met my spirit animals. The closer we come their white aura's grew brighter. Slowing down I could see Great Bear, White Wolf, Night Eagle, Fox and Crow.

"It's good to see all of you, I thought you had gone on vacation when I was having all this trouble," I snorted. I had felt betrayed in a small way, thinking they could have at least warned me about Roger.

"Good evening, Spirit Walker," said Great Bear. *"I hear a bit on hostility in your voice."*

"Maybe there is. I was wondering why you didn't warn me about Roger. Harley and I could have been killed."

"To get to the other side of the road sometimes we need to clear the obstacles in our way to gain our rewards that await us," spoke White Wolf.

"Rewards! Harley received one heck of a goose egg, I got snake bit and bruised ribs and a fellow student is dead."

Night Eagle flew down from his perch to a limb that put him eye level with me.

"Spirit Walker, the fall we did not anticipate but it also turned out to be for your own good. Harley only received a goose egg when hit on the back of his head, which should have killed him, and Roger chose the wrong road to walk down many years ago. He was an instrument which Shawgun used. We cannot protect you from every adversity, doing that you would not grow. You need those experiences," Night Eagle said adamantly.

"It's good to see you, Shadow," White Wolf said. *"We know you have always watched over Spirit Walker even before he knew you were one of his spirit animals. You've had your work cut out for you."*

"The demon that come out of the snake pit," Shadow addressed Crow, *"I haven't felt any lingering repercussions to Harley, will…"*

"No, he was a lower minion of Shawgun, sent only to retrieve the poison of the snake that bit Spirit Walker. Shawgun will use that as one of his weapons against him."

"Your real test has yet to begin and it is your impetuous nature that will get you into trouble but as in everything else you have to learn by experience," White Wolf paused to sit back on his haunches. *"The first snow will fall by morning. More will have fallen by the time you return home. But again it is not until the snow sticks to the side of the south face of the mountain."*

"Snow rarely sticks to that rock face." I stated.

"Then it will not be hard to know when you begin your hunt for Shawgun," Great Bear said.

"Do you have any other questions for us?" asked White Wolf.

"I'm assuming even though you do not answer when I call that you are still watching me?" I asked looking from one to the other.

"We will always watch over you, and give you answers but not as we are talking now. You have much to learn Spirit Walker and only though trail will you learn, unfortunately," White Wolf said smiling shaking his head.

******

"John I know there must be a secret to using this paint. Is it in the way you hold the brush?" I asked as I looked at the colors I had lain out and the three brushes besides the one I had in my hand.

"Each brush has a specific use, as each stroke of the brush leaves your creative impression.

On your pad practice your brush stokes before you attempt to paint your hawk," John answered as he demonstrated the different strokes with each brush.

I was amazed there was such a difference with each brush he used. More surprised that when I attempted to copy each stroke that John had done, mine looked like a duplicate. I know I sat there for an hour just doing brush strokes on my pad. Experimenting with different angles, light and heavier stokes, flares and single line widths. I was lost in the process and the patterns that flowed onto the sheet of paper.

"Kerry," spoke Harley, bringing me out of my trance.

"Sorry, what did you say," I asked rinsing off my brush before setting it down.

"Do you realize what you have painted?" He asked looking at one of my pages.

"No why I...," I stammered looking at the page Harley now held in his hand. It was the same markings that Roger had scratched in the dirt by the fire-pit at our camp. "I didn't realize that I'd painted them," I responded.

"We should hear back from my father tomorrow," he said looking puzzled. He placed the page under the others. "It's time for lunch."

"Shadow I noticed that you spent time with Garret this morning."

"Yes, he has a calming aura. The brothers compete against each other vigorously, but they have a great love and respect for each other. I will spend time with Aspen though I have sensed he has no real love for animals."

"Really, then why take a class on taxidermy I wonder. Will be interesting what you find out." I said following Harley into the dining room.

Mrs. Cantrell had made chicken pot pie and homemade bread. We picked up our meal from the long buffet table.

"Come Shadow," I heard her say. Shadow grinned and followed her out of the dining area.

"I don't know why but people fall in love with my dog."

"Shadow has a calming aura and he passes that on to those around him," commented Harley.

I held in my mind the picture of Red Tail Hawk as I started to paint the face of my bird. The strokes flowed and when I finished I saw that Mr. Chavez had been watching me.

"Well done, Kerry. As I have watched you it seems to me your talent appears when you go into a trace like state. I've never seen anyone do that before."

"I didn't realize I did that either. I know I focus and everything else around me vanishes into the background. I never thought of it as a trance."

"Does it happen in other area of your life?" he asked passing his hand over his goatee.

"With my photography I believe I use the same technique. I put all my energy into what I'm doing."

"We will have to talk sometime after class," he said and then moved onto another student.

Harley and I sat by the telephone waiting for it to ring. We were about to give up and go to our rooms when it rang.

"Father," Harley asked, excitedly.

"Yes, Father he's here by me," Harley said and put the phone so we could both listen to what Blue Heron had to say.

"Who found these marks?" Blue Heron asked.

"I did Sir. When we went back out to the camp site to take pictures," I answered.

"The symbols that you found are a warning that death awaits you. If you can learn how to unravel the spell you will break one of the links that gives Shawgun his strength and power."

"How will I do that Sir?"

"Spirit Walker only you can answer that. The answer will come from an unlikely source."

"Father, yesterday when Kerry was painting he drew the same symbols and he didn't even know that he had drawn them until I brought them to his attention," Harley remarked.

"It very well could come through a creative endeavor, one that the Creator could help with. Have you sought his direction, Spirit Walker?"

"Sir I'm afraid that I have not. I've relied on my spirit animals."

"Your spirit animals will always guide you, Spirit Walker, but they do not know all that the Great Spirit knows. He is boundless in his infinite wisdom, for he created all. You would be wise to keep him close," Blue Heron said reverently. "I do know this, Spirit Walker; you must have this accomplished before you seek out Shawgun."

I left Harley speaking with his father and I went to my room.

"Kerry, your aura is brown as a dirty river during a springtime melt. What did Blue Heron tell you?"

I felt the tears dropping from my eyes and I sat down heavily on my bed. Another weight added to my shoulders.

"Shadow, the markings are a death curse. I have to find a way to unravel the curse before I go after Shawgun. There is so much to do and so many lives at stake besides my own, I don't know if I can do this, Shadow," I said feeling heaviness in my chest. Moving automatically I removed my clothes and put my pajamas on. Sitting at the desk I looked over the pictures again hoping to stumble on to something we'd missed. There was nothing, but then again as tired as I was I could miss a bull standing in the pasture amongst the cows.

"You can do this. Moon Dancer knows you can do this. You have to have faith. The Great Spirit has not left you alone as he has given you your spirit guides, extraordinary gifts as he has great works for you to

accomplish. Those he has blessed with greatness he will put through the fire to refine. Now go to sleep," Shadow impressed upon my mind.

Today I would finish my bird and I was excited. The last touches would be put into place. As I finished my breakfast with, Harley and John, I had crossed John off my list of suspects.

Shadow hadn't felt any evil coming from Mr. Chavez so I could probably cross him off as well.

I thought of Rachael. Could she have found Roger or had she passed that information on to her brother Zeal/Dark Antelope. Shadow had not met Rachael and I wasn't sure if he would before we left for home. I thought about how adamant she'd been about me giving up Nakiya as Nakiya belonged to her brother.

"You ready," John asked rinsing his dish in the sink.

"Yes I am, how about you Harley. Your crow is looking great."

"I'm ready," Harley said and we filed out of the kitchen.

We still had a half hour before the other students would arrive but I decided not to wait or did Harley. I took out my Red Tail Hawk and set him at my work station. My paints and brushes I took out next and set beside my bird. I didn't pay attention to Harley now, as I focused on my own creation.

The last strokes of my brush had given him the finishing touch. I didn't know why but I laid my hand lightly on the back of my bird and closed my eyes.

I felt a tingling that started at my toes and move up through my body; the power and energy flowed through my hand that was touching the Red Tail Hawk. A light come forth from my fingers and spread around the bird and I would have sworn that I felt it breath under my hand. I stepped back and looked at my small creation and I held back the tears of joy as my eyes feasted on a dream come true.

"How did you do that, Kerry?" Harley asked coming to stand beside me. He looks like he could take flight. I've never seen a animal show that much life after being worked on. Indeed you have been blessed with a great gift."

"Could you touch mine, Kerry?"

"I don't know if it would work but I'll try," I said and walked over to where Harley's crow sat at his work station. I closed my eyes and felt the tingling start. As before a light came from my fingers and flowed over the crow. Harley stood in awe looking at his crow start to shimmer for a few seconds. "I don't know why, but I don't believe I could do that to anyone else's work, Harley."

John came out of the storage room and stopped in his tracks when he looked up and saw my hawk.

"Kerry...," he stopped in mid sentence as he looked at Harley's crow. "How...," he stammered again. "What did you do, how did you do...," he stammered again and walked around both birds and put his hand out timidly to touch one and then the other.

I really thought if he touched them they would fly away they looked so real, and so did John by the look on his face. I sat amazed that something had gone right; a dream had come true.

I couldn't wait for Jace and my family to see what I was capable of. At that moment I felt humble that Moon

Dancer and the Creator had given me such a wonderful gift.

******

It was a week until school would be over and my red tail hawk and Harley's crow was still the talk of the class. I couldn't reveal what happened nor could Harley, and John was still dumb founded. Mr. Chavez just smiled when he looked upon the birds like he knew what happened, he too remained silent.

It was Wednesday night when Mr. Chavez asked if he could talk to me alone. I invited him to my room.

"Kerry you know I'm not one for many words other than when I'm teaching. But I want to relate a story to you."

I motioned him to the chair and he sat down. I closed my door and sat down on my bed.

"When I was a young man my family lived on the border of Arizona and Mexico. I had two brothers and an older sister. She was beautiful beyond words and was loved by everyone. One day a band of renegade Indians rode through our village. The leader spied my sister as she walked home from the field from working. I saw the way he looked at her and I was afraid. The next morning my sister was missing. My brothers and my father went out searching for her. They found where she had been used for a human sacrifice, her body mutilated and then left for the wild animals. They brought back what was left of her body but they wouldn't let me or my mother see her before they buried her. I cried for her and then I started having nightmares."

I sat stunned at what I was hearing and knew it had to have been Shawgun that had sacrificed Mr. Chavez's sister.

"Then one night I went to my priest hoping he could help me get rid of my bad dreams. We prayed together and after he told me that one day I would meet a young man who could touch a dead animal and make it look alive. That young man would defeat the Indian who had sacrificed my sister. After that night I had no more nightmares. But I had a burning desire to learn taxidermy.

I felt it would be through that medium I would find him. And after all these years and giving up hope, here you sit."

I didn't know what to say when he finished his story. What could I say?

"When I walked into the classroom yesterday and saw your hawk and Harley's crow, I fought back my tears. I knew that her killer would soon be brought to justice, and my prayers would be answered."

"I don't know what to say Mr. Chavez."

"You need say nothing Kerry. You lived through two snake bites. I know you are the instrument that God will use to bring this murderer to justice. The priest said when I found you I was to give you this," he said taking out a piece of parchment from a book.

As I opened it up I fought the tears that threatened to intrude past my eyelids and my steal my calm demeanor. On the parchment was the symbols like the ones I found and another set which had to be the reversal to the curse. I just had to find out what each symbol meant. In smaller letters at the bottom was instruction of how to set the words for each symbol when I found them. The damn burst and my tears flowed and Mr. Chavez come over and sat beside me.

"Why you have been chosen for this task, I can't answer, only you know that. I know you'll accomplish it and hopefully you won't lose a love one in the process. I bid you good night, Kerry McDaniels."

I heard the door shut and Shadow laid his head on my lap.

"One door closes another one opens, does it not? We leave for home Saturday Kerry and your work will really start. But as you have seen there is always someone to help if you believe."

Friday night Harley came to my room to help me pack up my things and clean up the darkroom.

"Harley, you need to come to the ranch for Christmas. I don't know what your family does for Christmas but I really want you to come. Will you try?" I asked empting the developing solutions into a container. Harley took down the rest of the pictures that I left hanging.

"I will talk to my father, Kerry."

We looked at the photos again and at the ones Harley had just taken down. I kept coming back to the one of the snake that had its fangs removed. There was something about it I couldn't let go of. I just didn't know what it was.

"How's your head, Harley where Roger hit you?" I asked putting the picture away with the ones I wanted to keep separated from the rest.

Harley rolled his eyes at me as he handed me the photos.

"You wouldn't know there had been a goose egg."

"You used one of your concoctions. Why wouldn't you, they worked great on me."

"Yes I did. It was gone before you left the hospital."

"You're father must be a great healer to teach you so well," I said putting the pictures in my suitcase.

"Actually, it was my mother who taught me about herbs and how to use them. She works alongside my father. I guess you could say they are a team for almost forty years now."

I checked the darkroom again to make sure I had taken everything out and then shut the door. I opened my other suitcase and placed it on the chair.

"Do your brothers help in the store your family has?" I asked moving to the window. Snow had started falling again. There was about two feet on the ground already, so I knew there could be double that amount if not more at home.

"I hope the snow stops. Do they clear the road you travel home on?"

"They try. But if they close the road my brothers will come get me with the dog sleds. I'm thinking the sun will be out tomorrow and I shouldn't have any trouble getting home. I'm not as far away as you. If I came for Christmas I will ride the train more than likely. You asked about my brothers. They do help in the store and they also have a band they have put together. They're really pretty good, but I don't tell them that." He said and we laughed.

Shadow, Harley, John and I stood on the train platform. Harley had been right about the sun coming up. It had warmed to just above freezing. He had checked

286

earlier on road conditions and was told the road was open that took him home. We listened to the train whistle as it came into town a mile from the station.

The baggage handler put my suitcases in the baggage car. I carried my camera case and my Red Tail Hawk that I had under a cloth cover.

"Thank you, John, I really enjoy the classes. If you ever make it up our way you best stop by the ranch," I said shaking his gloved hand.

I looked around, swallowed hard to control my emotions.

"I'll see you at Christmas, right Harley." I took his hand then pulled him in for a McDaniels hug. I felt very close to Harley. When you go through experiences with someone, good or bad it seems to bring you closer together. And Harley and I had some of both.

Shadow followed me up the steps of the train car. He laid down on the floor, and the seat next to me I set my camera bag, but I held my hawk. I saw John come up the stairs.

"Kerry I almost forgot. Rachel sent you something to snack on," he said handing me a sack.

"Tell her thanks. Take care, John." I turned to look out the window and waved at Harley. I had a gut feeling I would see him at Christmas.

"I will miss him, Shadow."

Chapter SIXTEEN

We were ten miles out of Havre when it started to snow again. The white winter wonder land was indeed beautiful. The snow sparkled like diamonds across the prairie. Watching the snow fall made me tired and I felt myself dozing. I placed the hawk beside my camera case afraid I would drop it when I fell asleep. And sleep we did.

It was around two p.m., when we pulled into Libby. It was great to see my hometown. Every shop window was decorated for Christmas and on the street corners were speakers and Christmas music played. I looked around for my ride and didn't see any of the trucks. I gathered my things and woke up Shadow.

"We're home Shadow," I said moving my legs so he could get to the isle. The sun was shining and rays danced across the newly fallen snow giving off a prism light show. The trees dressed in their winter gowns glistened and sparkled waiting for a grand ball to start as mom would say.

"Looks like no one is here yet, Shadow. Let's walk down to Mr. Granger's café. I could use a piece of huckleberry pie. How about you?"

"I'll pass on the pie but maybe he'll have a rib or two." He smiled showing his white teeth.

"I bet he will," I answered looking around for Chuck who transported the luggage. "Oh Chuck can I leave my luggage here until Dad comes to get me? I will take my backpack."

"Sure thing Kerry. I'll put it in the back of the stock room."

"Thanks," I waved and started down the street that had been partially cleared to the café. I was glad I had worn my snow boots. They were warmer than my other ones.

Walking into Mr. Granger's Café the bells chimed and it looked festive decorated in green and red. There was a Christmas tree standing in the back corner by the fire place. He had decorated the tree with new bulbs that looked like candles and bubbles run up and down in the thin cylinder. Tinsel that had been carefully laid over branches reflected the color of the shiny red, green and blue ornaments. Atop was an angel holding a golden harp and the tree skirt was a Christmas scene that lay under several packages. The tip of each branch had been flocked with imitation snow. The fireplace was draped with garland and mistletoe hung over several tables. The jute that held the bells on the front door had been replaced with red satin ribbon.

"Go lay on the rug by the fireplace Shadow," I said taking off my gloves moving toward the counter. "Mr. Granger."

"Kerry, I'm glad to see you made it with that storm we had last night I didn't know if the tracks would be clear over the pass."

"Yep, we're back," I said glancing over at Shadow.

"You wouldn't happen to have a piece of huckleberry pie would ya?" I asked sitting up to the counter.

"I sure do. I may complain about putting them up in the summer but I'm sure happy when winter comes and I have them to make my pie. Just a minute and I'll get you a piece."

"That storm must have been a bad one if Bob and Harold aren't sitting in here."

"Well I guess no one told you being away and all," he said setting down the pie and a glass of milk. He then walked over to Shadow and gave him something in some tin foil.

"I guess it wasn't long after you left that old Bob caught pneumonia and a week later he died and I've not seen Harold since. People around town say they won't be surprised if Harold don't make it through the winter," he said patting Shadow on top of his head.

"That's too bad. I liked listening to their stories," I said and then took a bit of pie. I relished the flavor as it run over my tongue and down my throat. Mmm this is good."

"What's under the cloth?" he asked while he poured him a bit of ginger ale, which he used for indigestion.

"Well I'll show you and you are the first Mr. Granger," I said as I took the black cloth off my Red Tail Hawk. I heard him gasp.

"Oh my dirty britches, will you look at that. Are you sure he's stuffed, Kerry?" He asked looking at the bird from several different angles. "If I saw him on the porch I'd swear he was real and was going to lift up and fly. Wait till folks get a look at him."

I finished my pie while Mr. Granger sat and studied my hawk.

"Oh before I forget, your pa said for you to stay in town tonight and he'd be in in the morning to get you. And that your company arrived safely."

"I'd better call him," I said rushing to the phone.

"You can't call. The lines are down. I was lucky to talk to your dad before they went dead."

"Mr. Granger, can I leave my stuff here?" I asked pulling on my gloves.

"Where you going, Kerry?" he asked as his forehead creased tighter.

"I'm going home. Nakiya is here."

"Kerry, that ain't such a good idea. We could get more snow tonight," he said nervously walking around the counter.

"The sun is out and if I take the short cut I'll be home in no time," I said reaching down to retrieve the foil that had held shadow's treat.

"I think you should listen to Mr. Granger about this Kerry," Shadow said standing up.

"That's another whole day, Shadow. I'm going now. If you want to stay here I'm sure Mr. Granger won't care," I snorted walking toward the door.

"I'll put your things in the back room, Kerry. Sure you won't change your mind. Your Dad is going to skin me alive for letting you take off in this weather," he grumbled picking up my things.

"Coming Shadow," I asked holding the door open letting the winter cold flow into the room.

"I'm coming but letting you know that actions like this always gets you into trouble," he said crossing over the threshold into the cold.

"Look Shadow, the sun is out the sky is blue and if we take the short cut by the cave we'll be home in no time," I said thinking only of seeing Nakiya.

"That may be true for the moment, Kerry. You know how fast the weather changes out here," Shadow said trotting up beside me. *"At least slow down, tramping through this snow is going to tire you out faster than if you go at a slower steady pace."*

"Okay, you're probably right about that," I agreed watching him struggle to keep up with me. It was only four miles to the ranch taking this shortcut.

We'd made it a mile and a half when the clouds started to roll in. Not just any clouds, but dark heavy clouds and a light breeze filtered through the trees. I tripped on a hidden fallen branch and then I remember this area. It had massive dead fall on this side of the river. I would have to go slower watching where I stepped.

"Be extra careful through here Shadow. Remember all the dead fall," I said and then it registered the snow was deeper in here looking at how far I sunk with each step. The sun during the day wouldn't reach it enough to melt. "Follow in my footstep and that will help you, Shadow."

The wind picked up and the trees danced their own graceful dance and the snow started to fall. I wondered if the sun didn't make it down here why was the snow making its way. The intensity rose as the wind howled bowing limbs kicking up the light snow to obscure my vision. I heard branches break under the assault and when looking around I slipped on a branch. Startling me and a buck that had been watching us from the shadows, I missed the tree I went to grab for and fell.

My scream was hushed under the impregnable wind.

"Kerry, what did you do," Shadow shouted coming around to the front of me.

"I think when I fell a stick went into my leg." I pushed away the snow and watched as the white turned crimson red.

"Can you pull your leg up," asked Shadow trying to keep me calm.

"I don't think so, but I'll try," I answered pulling up slightly till the pain took my vision, and for a moment I swayed making me lose my other foot hold and I fell sideward's. Snap! I felt the stick break. I was clutching for the light. I couldn't let go of the light.|

"Kerry, listen to me Kerry. Open your eyes," I faintly heard Shadow say, but I felt him lick my face. I'd fallen into deeper snow that now covered part of my body. I couldn't stay here. I knew that as I tried to find something sturdy to pull myself up with.

"Kerry above your head there is a limb I believe will hold your weight. Try to reach it."

I pushed up with one arm as I grab for the branch wrapping my fingers around it. Trying to shut out the pain I pulled myself up into a standing position. The stick was lodge into my thigh.

"If you try to pull it out now, you'll bleed to death," Shadow exclaimed.

I reached for my backpack.

"My backpack, can you see my backpack, Shadow?" It was snowing harder and I knew if this kept up we'd lose our way to the cave. I'd already lost my direction. I had to depend on Shadow to get us there before dark which didn't give us much time.

"You left it at Mr. Grangers, Kerry. We're not too far from the river and the cave. You can do this so don't dwell

on the backpack, it's not here but we're close to shelter. Can you see a small limb you can use for a crutch?"

"Yes," I said pulling it up through the snow. This will work." The snowed packed into my pants had slowed the bleeding down. Cautiously I followed Shadow the excruciating pain flooded my mind with a red burst of light.

I could feel the snow numbing my leg with each step I took and wished it would do the same with the pain. I was thinking we were nearly clear of the worst deadfall if only the snow would let up and the wind would quit.

Why hadn't I listened especially with so much at stake? I was surprised I hadn't heard from Moon Dancer, but he might be frozen, I know my ears felt like they had fallen off even with my hood up.

I could hear the river as we were getting closer.

"Shadow?"

"We are almost to the river Kerry. How is the leg?" he asked weaving around the last of the deadfall.

"I can't feel it too much. I think the snow around it has frozen the nerves in that area."

Instead of the snow slowing and the wind stopping it brought in another assault. I was glad Shadow and I spoke telepathically otherwise I wouldn't have heard him. I barely heard the tree crash behind me, and I didn't look around to see just how close it had come to taken me with it.

"Kerry, I smell evil in the wind, hurry if you can." Shadow spoke standing on the river bank. *"Remember the old tree that lay across the river?"* he asked looking back at me as I tried to maneuver my leg faster.

"Yes I remember. I don't know how sturdy it is. It's been there a long time, Shadow." I stopped next to him unable to see further than across the river. I knew Shadow couldn't cross the span and stay dry other than the tree bridging this side to the other.

"You go ahead. You're lighter that I am."

He didn't stall; we didn't have time to figure out other options. I watched him slowly make his way across to the other side and my heart gladden. If I didn't make it at least he would have the cave to get in out of the weather.

"I'm not sure I can make it across walking," I said patting the snow down. It wasn't a small log that had fallen years ago but it wasn't a large one either. I could wrap my arms around it. I patted the snow as far as I could reach safely, rather than pushing it off making the bark like ice.

"Use your stick for balance, Kerry," Shadow stated laying in the snow in front of the log trying to make it into a solid area.

"Looking down at the inch round stick perturbing out of my leg turned my stomach upside down. I was sure it was the huckleberry pie that was trying it make its way back up. Looking at the river this was the narrowest place to cross. There were some ice covered spots but they would be thin layered. There were too many rocks up and down the river and two much water for it to freeze.

I placed my left leg up on the log feeling like it was a solid step. Pushing off on the stick I brought my right leg up and balanced, before I placed it in front of my left leg and supported my weight with the small branch I used for a cane. I felt a slight disturbance as the log moved slightly at the end I was standing on and held my breath. I couldn't step back that wasn't an option.

"Shadow if I fall you take cover in the cave until this storm quits," I said wishing I had my goggles on to keep the snow out of my eyes. The snow Shadow had flattened had another layer of snow on it already. I took a second step wanting to scream as my weight shifted to my injured leg. A wave of dizziness swept over me.

"Kerry, take another step," Shadow urged. I could feel his intense stare on me. *"Come on another step. Think of Nakiya waiting for you at the ranch.*

Finding my balance I took the step and felt another shift of the log.

"Breathe, Spirit Walker. What is happening now," voiced Moon Dancer in my head.

"Not now Moon Dancer. I can't explain right now I have to concentrate."

"Then breathe while you're doing it. We both need oxygen." I heard his concern but he kept silent.

I braced my cane in front and slowly moved my injured leg ahead of my other one. I was closer. The wind rage on and I wasn't sure if it would be the log slipping or the wind blowing me off the darn thing that would be my demise. I was glad that my steps had sunk into a grove of the tree helping me with my balance. I tried to put more weight on the cane as I shifted to my good leg. This time I did cry out the pain so intense at this point I didn't care if I fell or not. The image of Nakiya appeared in my mind, she was holding out her hands…

"Come to me Kerry, I'm waiting for you."

I took a few short breaths and took another step reaching out to take her hands. I was almost there.

Feeling my weight shift I dropped my cane as the log gave way swinging into the bank I was approaching. My arms flung around the tree and as it hit the embankment my leg swung down hitting the tree pushing the stick through to the other side of my leg. I felt Shadow grip my coat with his teeth and then something else gripped my other side pulling me up onto the bank as the tree broke its hold going into the water and was carried downstream. The wind howled with vengeance through the swinging trees.

"Nakiya!" I screamed and then saw Shawgun laughing at me. *Eyes, open eyes, my words floated away from me and I wanted to follow them. I wanted to fill*

peaceful and warm; I wanted Nakiya she was just ahead of me, waiting. I tried running but once again the faster I ran I couldn't close the gap between us.

The snow was so cold on my face and I couldn't brush it off, something was holding my arms. Was I moving? My stomach felt like it, I was going to be sick. Something pulled my hood back, it was so cold.

"Spirit Walker, listen to me. Spirit Walker listen to me!"

"Moon Dancer is that you? I just want to go to sleep, let me sleep."

"Spirit Walker, open your eyes. You can't sleep. Open your eyes. We have too much to do."

"I'm too tired; let me sleep for just a little while until the pain goes away."

"No!" Screamed Moon Dancer.

I felt like I had a sonic boom go off inside my head.

"Spirit Walker you have to remove the stick from you leg"

The voice in my head was so loud I tried to block it out. I just want to sleep, I'm so cold.

What's licking my face, *"Is that you Shadow?"*

"Kerry open your eyes, you can't go to sleep. If you go to sleep you'll never see Nakiya and she's waiting at the ranch for you right now. You need to listen to Moon Dancer."

My eyes fluttered but I couldn't see light.

"Shadow I can't see. I have my eyes open but I can't see."

"Kerry we are in the cave. Brother Wolf and I pulled you in here."

"It's so quite."

"The wind stopped and there is only a light snowfall since we entered the cave."

"We took the stash home."

"There is still a small stack of firewood if you can get it started it will warm you."

Feeling around in my pockets I found my train ticket that would help if only I could find some matches. Inside my coat pocket my fingers brush a book of matches and I pulled it out. It wasn't full.

"Shadow can you drag the wood over here. I might as well been blind. The snowfall on the big blue spruce pine stopped any light coming in, but then I couldn't remember if there would be a moon tonight anyway.

My hearing was still in tack as I heard the once stacked firewood being dropped in front of me.

"Shadow is Brother Wolf still here?"

"Yes, Spirit Walker I'm still here."

I felt him lick the side of my face.

"Thank you, Thank you both for getting me inside the cave," I said feeling his warm pelt I put my arms around him.

"Is this enough to start the fire," asked Shadow.

Feeling for the stack of sticks I took my train ticket and squished it up placing it under the dry wood. The paper ticket caught with the second match and flared.

Blowing gently it ignited the firewood. I gave Shadow and Brother Wolf a grim smile.

"Spirit Walker while you have light you need to look at your leg. The stick needs to come out," stated Moon Dancer.

I unzipped my jacket getting the bulk away from the front of me and put my scarf to the side. I was surprised my pants weren't torn other than where the stick entered through my jeans and long-johns.

"The only way I'm going to see the damage you guys, is to take my jeans down. I think my leg is numb because right now the pain is minimal. How much firewood do we have Shadow?"

"Not enough to last the night, so you better be quick doing what you gotta do." He replied.

I laid back and peeled my jeans over my hips and then sat up when I realized the stick would have to come out first. I lay back down and pulled them up cringing at my legs rejection of movement. Reaching down I felt the stick and the knob that had been pushed through my leg; the knob that acted as a barb preventing me from pulling it out.

My fingers traced the protruding object and I didn't think I could pull it out straight.

"Shadow you are going to have to help me. I can't pull this all the way out," I said scratching behind his ears.

"What do you want me to do?" Was Shadow's simple reply.

"I'm going to hold my leg up and you need to pull the stick out. Straight out if you can."

Rising up my leg as high as I could, I felt a trickling of blood before Shadow clamped down and in one motion he pulled the stick out. My scream vibrated through the cave and out into the night breaking the silence that had settled over the area. Blood was now a steady stream running down my leg. Feeling sick again I leaned over, my sides contracted and my thought of huckleberry pie would never be the same again. My head was swimming, but I forced my eyes to stay open.

"Spirit Walker you need to cauterize your wound," Moon Dancer said as he was still very much awake.

I rolled back over. Oh no, I don't want to do that. I had seen Jace cauterize wounds on the ranch. Maybe I could do one, but two. The first one I would probably pass out. The fire was dwindling. If I was going to do this I had to do it now.

"Spirit Walker I will lend you my strength to get you through this." I heard Moon Dancer say.

After pushing my jeans back down I pushed myself up into a sitting position and used my scarf as a tourniquet. I knew the blood should have pushed out any foreign matter, but I had to take care of things on the outside.

I put a piece of wood between my teeth and picked up the stick that had only been burning on one end. Bracing my leg against the cave wall I touched the hot end of the stick to the wound.

My burning flesh sizzled and the smell of the burnt flesh turned my stomach over. I laid the stick back in the fire and then pushed the flesh together biting down on the stick until I thought my teeth would bite though. My breathing came in gasps.

"Hurry now the other opening." Moon dancer urged.

I picked up the stick and touched the front wound opening. The stick snapped. Shadow licked my cheek catching the tears that ran.

Wrapping my scarf around my leg I eased my jeans back up and zipped up my coat. The fire gave off a soft glow.

"Is there wood left on the pile," I asked Shadow.

"This is the end of it Kerry."

What little warmth there was in the cave was dissipating. I sat between Brother Wolf and Shadow capturing the heat from their bodies. I didn't know what time it was or how soon help would come. I think I told Mr. Granger I was taking the short cut and Jace would know what short cut I meant.

Even with the warmth of the animals my legs were cold. With the help of Moon Dancer I was tolerating the pain, but just as it fogged my thinking.

I heard the call of the first wolf and Brother Wolf sat up. It was only minutes later I heard something push past the pine branches. Brother Wolf moved to the opening of the cave.

"It is my mate. She is afraid to enter but come to warn me of the danger," He said.

We listened to the small whimpers for a few minutes before I heard her leave and Brother Wolf come back and sat beside me.

"It's your blood that calls to the pack," he said.

I left a blood trail on the other side of the river as well as this side and it led right into the cave. I had no gun, heck I couldn't walk even if I tried to make the other two miles to home I'd have to crawl. Our only advantage was the blue spruce that blocked the cave entrance so the wolves couldn't make a full frontal assault. Shadow and Brother Wolf were my only protection from a pack of hungry wolves.

"These are not just hungry wolves, Kerry. Evil runs amongst them," Shadow stated.

I felt both of my kindred friends tense. Tears filled my eyes. *Why had I been so impetuous? How many would have to suffer or die before I learned to be patient. I caught a sob, crying isn't going to get me out of this situations, I didn't know what was. I had so many that trusted me and what did I do, act like a love sick calf for someone who I could never call my own anyway. Get a grip Kerry,* I scolded myself.

I felt around the cave floor looking for any kind of a weapon. We heard them coming. My hand slid over cold metal and grab hold. It was the small shovel I brought in this summer to dig the hole for my stash. I didn't fill quite as helpless. I forced myself onto my knees ignoring the pain that poured into my leg up to my hip. I wasn't going to die here I had a mission I had to finish.

My body froze in place when we heard the snarls outside the cave. It sounded like so many. A patch of snow fell from a branch as the first wolf made his way to the entrance. Shadow and Brother Wolf growled a warning and Brother Wolf made the first move leaping at the wolf.

I tried to communicate with the pack but it was like they had a barrier up I couldn't get through. Shawgun, Shawgun controlled these wolves that was the only explanation.

A second wolf entered and targeted Shadow. I was afraid to swing the shovel not being able to see which animal I struck. I might as well have been without anything. The fought savagely, I was knocked over and my leg stepped on. I was bit in my calf as I pulled myself away and into the small nook. Growls, snarls, rang against the cave walls. I could smell blood and I was sure that it was from all four animals. Crouched in front of me I saw red eyes glow. I hadn't heard the third wolf enter as the fighting raged.

I held the shovel up as the wolf attacked bringing it down on the animals shoulder with all the strength I could muster. I felt it slice through flesh and the animal screamed. I wasn't sure how many more entered but I knew Shadow was badly hurt. Teeth ripped into my coat and flesh as feathers floated around my head and into my mouth. I fought to hold on to the shovel keeping the animal away from my throat. That's when I hear it; a gunshot.

Chapter SEVENTEEN

One of the wolves was shot, the yelp triggered a retreat. Enraged snarls ricocheted through the trees as bullets hit their target.

I brought the shovel down with one hand with all my strength and some from Moon Dancer's into the wolf's neck. Blood flew hitting me in the face as the wolf slumped over my body.

"Kerry! Kerry!" I heard someone yell. I pushed the wolf off me to reach Shadow and Brother Wolf.

"Shadow, Brother Wolf," I drugged myself along the cave floor feeling for my friends.

"Kerry answer me, son," I heard Dad yell.

"I'm in here Dad. I'm in the cave." I sobbed. Shadow and Brother Wolf seemed to be lifeless when I reached them.

"Dad is Jace with you?" I called out when I saw the light shine through the pine tree.

"Kerry, he's right behind me." Dad said entering the cave shining the light into my face. I knew I must be covered with blood and the feathers from my down jacket.

"Jace, Shadow and Brother Wolf saved my life you have to help them," I cried. A third light entered the cave.

"Can't you stay out of trouble?" Josh asked looking at me and then over at Brother Wolf.

I heard Brother Wolf whine and then growl.

"Brother Wolf, do not fear these men. They will not harm you. They are going to help you. Please allow them to assist you and thank you for protecting me."

"I will trust them, for I trust your word," Brother Wolf said.

I pulled myself over to Shadow and ran my hand through his blood soaked coat.

"Shadow, Shadow, answer me," I called to him. I felt him touch my mind, but that was all.

"Kerry they are both in bad shape," Jace said. We need to get them back to the ranch, now!

"How bad are you hurt, Son?"

"I'm bad, but not as bad as they are." I replied. I heard another gunshot and then two more. "Who else is with you?"

"Both your brothers and it was Jace that suggested we bring the sleds. Here, let's get this blood wiped off your face. You don't want your mother seeing you like this. How bad is that wolf bite on your arm?" he asked wiping clean my face of blood and feathers with his neckerchief.

"I'm not sure Dad I hurt in so many places at this moment, but it's my leg I'm most worried about. I put a stick through my right thigh."

Dad just shook his head. "Jace when you get Shadow out of here yell at one of your brothers to come help me with Kerry," He requested watching Jace and Josh with Shadow working their way back out through the pine branches.

"Leave your coat on we can look at the bite when we get you home. It's too cold. I can't remember when the temperature had plummeted like it did tonight."

"Here, you need some help, Little Brother," Steve said grinning. "When are we going to stop rescuing you?"

They both hooked me under my arms and pulled me up and I let out a cry that was heard outside the cave. Dipping under the opening to the cave I released a second cry. Perhaps I should have put a stick in my mouth to silence the groans I made. It was too late now. They'd all think I was a wimp. They sat me in the sled with Shadow and covered us up with a wool blanket.

"Josh," I caught his attention bringing out Brother Wolf. "I need to speak to you." He nodded and continued to the other sled to lay Brother Wolf on the seat. Dad was getting in his saddle. "Josh, the other wolf in the cave that I killed, I think you should burn it. It had red eyes of a demon."

"I agree. I'll take care of it," he said rubbing his gloved hand over Shadow's muzzle.

Rob came back and stopped his horse by the sled.

"Those are the first wolves that after being shot at turned around to attack again. We had to kill five of them. I didn't see anymore. I sure don't want Anderson to know about this as he's always looking for reason to get rid of the wolves in Montana. This incident would add fuel to his fire."

316

"Let's get you home," Dad said looking to see if everyone was ready.

"I'll be along in just a minute," Josh said. "Go on ahead."

As I was sitting in the sled looking at where we had come from I saw the flames light up the night. I and everyone else heard the wrenching scream of Shawgun. Shadow raised his head slightly and Jace turned around and looked at me. Dad, Rob and Steve stopped their horses. All had questioning looks wondering what had made the horrible freighting sound. But no one said anything they just picked up their pace toward home.

*"Shadow I believe we fought with demons, this night."*I said

"Is that suppose to make me feel better," he said solemnly closing his eyes.

"Yes. Because you fought wolves with super natural strength and we survived. I apologized for putting you both in harm's way."

"Then do us all a favor and stay on task," reprimanded Moon Dancer.

I said nothing because I knew he was right and that's what I had to do. I saw Josh coming up the rear in the other sled at a fast trot and I relaxed knowing he and Brother Wolf were safe from Shawgun, hopefully everyone would be.

Mom was pacing outside on the porch bundled up, she must have heard the sleigh bells coming home. We pulled up in front of the small vet hospital and she flew into my arms. But from her shocked expression on her face Dad must not have done a good job of removing all the blood.

"Kerry, whatever possessed you to try and walk home in winter knowing how fast the weather can change," she scolded. "Mr. Granger called us as soon as the telephones were working again.

Dad and Steve helped me out of the sled and into the hospital. I looked at that hard steel table not relishing the thought of lying on it again as I had from the gunshot wound in July. Jace and Josh brought in Shadow and then Brother Wolf. At the looks of them in the light they had lost a lot of blood because their coats were covered crimson red.

"Alright, young man." When I heard that tone of voice from Mom there would be no argument to what she wanted to know.

"Let's get those pants off so I can see the damage," she stated.

I removed my jacket and heard her gasp at the ugly bite mark as my shirt was torn and bloody. Taking off my jeans I thought she was going to pass out when she saw the damage to my thigh.

"Jacob, we need Doc. If you don't think one of the trucks will make it you'll need to take the sleigh but we need him out here as soon as possible."

"We'll get Doc, Sally. Right now why don't you get an antiseptic and clean that wolf bite." Dad said.

It was the first time I'd seen my mom unraveled and my dad, take over.

"You need some help in here?" I heard Danene ask. I looked over to see her and Nakiya come through the door.

I grabbed the blanket and threw it over my lower body.

"My gosh, Kerry what happened to you," Danene asked rushing over to me her eyes wide open. "You look like you've been under a bucking bronco.

"Yes, what happened Kerry?" Nakiya asked the same thing a catch in her voice.

She come and stood beside me and picked up my hand. My insides instantly went soft as a marshmallow and my heart fluttered.

"Kerry, this emotional train is what got us into trouble?" Scolded Moon Dancer. *"If you are going to save her, tighten your bow string.*

"You're right," I said taking back my hand to clutch my blanket that I made appear to be slipping.

Mom sensed my discomfort. "Danene, why don't you girls go back to bed? We're going to be a here while and there is no sense in all of us losing sleep."

"Okay Mom. Dad how is Shadow?" With the other curtain pulled she didn't see Brother Wolf. He was nervous enough being around all these humans and it was only Josh's ability with animals that would kept him calm.

"I'm sure sis with some rest and Jace's nurturing he'll be fine," Rob said and pulled the curtain around the table.

"I'll talk to you later, Kerry," Nakiya said walking toward the door waiting for Danene to leave with her.

Danene picked up on the tension in the room and left quickly.

"Jace this wolf is going to need some blood." Josh said coming around the curtain his lips pressed tight.

"In the fridge you'll find an ample supply."

"I'll need a sedative also. I can feel his apprehension I think he's worried about his mate. I noticed she followed us in. She'll be alright won't she?" Josh asked lowering his voice. "I know she will stay out of sight but if she can feel his stress she might venture in closer."

"I'll tell my ranch hands in the morning to watch for her. They all know we don't shoot wolves on Rose Feather," Dad said sternly with a furrowing brow. All of you, what happened out there tonight will not go outside this room,"

"What do you mean what happened. There's something you're not telling Jacob?" Mom asked turning my dad toward her. "What aren't you telling me?"

"We'll talk later Sally. Doc is waiting for me."

I felt like things were coming to a head and I wasn't sure how I was going to explain it without risking Moon Dancer and my quest. I knew I was in trouble when Mom came over with the antiseptic bottle in one hand, gauze in the other; and the look that said 'let's have it'. I'd been deserted as my brothers had gravitated over to Shadow's table and pulled the curtain shut again.

"I think it's time we had a talk don't you," she asked dousing the gauze with antiseptic. "How did you get this bite?" she paused a moment her eyes blinking rapidly waiting for me to answer and when I didn't she continued. "All the time I've lived on this ranch I've never know anyone who's been bitten by a wolf."

"Mom it was the smell of blood from my leg that drew the pack," I said as beads of sweat formed across my forehead.

The cold had numbed most of the pain when I was outside, but now I was agonizing. The only thing that took the edge off was the way Mom looked at me with her stormy blue eyes and rubbed the wet gauze around the bite and not too gently I must say.

"I see. You wouldn't mind explaining the reason you brought one home with you to mend after he attacked you."

"Well, Brother Wolf is special Mom and he wasn't part of the pack that attacked us." I said tearing the rest of my shirt sleeve off that was already beyond repair. Her eyebrows come together and she pressed a little harder around that wolf bite. I cringed not wanting to cry out. And at this point I wasn't sure what hurt worse my leg or the bite she was trying to scrub away. She eased up when she saw my eyes watering.

"And why is this wolf you call Brother Wolf special?" she asked her hand shaking sliding the blanket off my leg enough to expose the burnt flesh. She laid down the bloody gauze pad and pulled her long red hair back and fastened it with a barrette she took out of her pocket. "I'll leave this until doc gets here. Go on, I'm listening."

I was starting to chill again, the pain from my thigh raced all the way to my hip. I lay back and gritted my teeth.

"Shadow, are you going to be alright," I asked hoping to get an answer. He had every right to be upset with me.

"Mom, please ask how Shadow and Brother Wolf are doing. It's my fault and if…"

She walked over to the table before I finished saying anything else and I closed my eyes. I was getting sick again which was strange because there was nothing left in my stomach to come up.

"It's going to be a while until they know. Both animals have lost a lot of blood, and Jace and Josh are working as fast as they can to sew up tears'. Their injuries aren't like a knife cut."

"Now tell me about Brother Wolf."

"Brother Wolf is the wolf I saved from one of Anderson's traps. Shadow and I have been friends with him ever since that day."

"I heard Josh say that his mate is close by," she said wiping the moisture from my face. "She must be hungry.

I'll find something for her to eat later and toss it out to her. She'll be able to worry easier on a full stomach.

I pulled the blanket up under my chin and heard someone put more wood in the pot belly stove that usually kept the small hospital cozy. I was so tired I just wanted to sleep and so cold I couldn't quit shaking.

"Mom, I need a bucket," I called to her trying to lean over the edge of the table. I was so weak.

"Rob, come help me!" Her shrill voice brought him over immediately as she grabbed me to keep me from falling.

I felt strong hands hold me on to the table and someone put a cold wash cloth on the back of my neck. After I heaved the bile I couldn't open my eyes and I agonized as the pain ripped through my body. The wolf bite felt like my arm was on fire and all I could see were red eyes laughing at me. I think I drifted in and out of sleep, because I could hear voices around me, hands touching me.

"Mom, I'm so cold," I mumbled looking at the foggy images.

Words were forming in my mind and colors swirled in intricate pattern around them. I was trying to make sense of the meaning when the green, gray and tan colors merged. I felt my heart stop for a moment as the colors slither toward me. The snake raised its head and our eyes made contact.

"Spirit Walker, rushing things again I see," said Snake my newest spirit animal.

I didn't know why I knew him but I knew Snake was my eighth spirit animal and that we had met before as memories flooded my mind with information.

"I remember we met at the bottom of the snake pit. You bit me twice," I said.

Seeing Moon Dancer come from his slumber place in my mind, he sat beside me.

"Your quite place is serene, Kerry," Moon Dancer said looking around. *"Why haven't you showed this to me before?"* He asked nodding slowly.

"I thought with you in my mind you would know everything about me," I confessed and watched him turn to Snake.

"Greetings Snake, I see our impetuous friend has once more interrupted your time table."

"Sometimes the Great Spirit has his own time table as we have seen many times. The reason is not for us to question but to go with the flow as I've heard them say. I don't know why many of your adventures include pain, Spirit Walker, I will leave that between you and the Great Spirit," Snake said swaying back and forth causing me to enter a hypnotic state.

I looked around the quite place I'd made in my mind when I wanted to meditate. I heard the splashing current of the stream, inhaled the scent of pine and sagebrush, and heard the occasional song of a meadowlark as I sat crossed leg on a rock overlooking a small wildflower filled meadow.

"Your quite place will help you through this trauma as you purge the poison from your body. The pain will be severe; your loved ones with the exception of the healers will think you dead. Truthfully, without Snake Medicine you would be dead already. The poison from the snake in the pit has been laced with demon blood making it a powerful killer. Shawgun wants you dead and each act that you do without thinking of the consequences opens the

door for him to get to you," Snake finished and coiled down."

"Will Moon Dancer be safe?" I asked worried about his energy being weakened more that it was.

"As long as Moon Dancer stays in this place he'll be fine. In fact it will be Moon Dancer that will hold you here when you hear the cries from your loved ones. From this place, follow the poison with your inner eyes as it runs through your body. You will push it back out through the wolf bite; your body will feel like it's a glacier as you lay motionless."

"Running Wolf is now mixing herbs that will help pull the poison out," Moon Dancer added clenching his jaw afterward.

"What about Shadow and Brother Wolf. They were bitten, will they die?" I asked soberly rocking back and forth on my rock.

"Their bites were only demon possessed so it will depend on the skill of the healer," Snake responded. "We must start. The longer the poison stays in your body the harder it will be for you to transmute and expel," Snake informed me looking into my eyes again.

I felt I was submerging into the very rock I sat upon but I kept my feeling of calm.

At first I watched the dark green substance calmly flow trying to merge with my blood. The words I'd seen earlier, unscrambled, formed and I started to chant.

"*May-say-hash-div-mahatma-say-sol-div*", as I repeated the words again, Moon Dancer joined me. The substance quivered changing a shade lighter with teeny tiny spikes emerging, the substance assaulted the tissue around my lungs. The pain was staggering. Through my heart flowed a clear substance with my blood that was so cold that when it surrounded the first green liquid it turned it to slush. But before the clear liquid could capture all the green substance the spikes ran before it attacking the cells in its path trying to escape. The tiny spikes punctured the walls of my veins as it raced to my vital organs trying to do as much damage before the clear substance and healing light could turn it to a harmless slush. My body convulsed and I was freezing while the cold substance chased the tiny spikes to the entrance of the wolf bite.

Feeling my body shut down as we trailed behind the clear substance, I heard my mother cry out and then start to sob. My attention went to the outside of my body. Josh and Nakiya were chanting but I couldn't understand the words. Mom watched Josh administer herbs that Nakiya had been mixing in a bowl. My body stilled all functions to use its energy to push the poison out. The clear fluid semi- froze the poison delivering the waste to the herbs that pulled it through the gaping hole and out of my body.

I tried to open my eyes so my mother didn't think me dead as my body felt ice cold. Moon Dancer pulled me back into my mind.

"No Spirit Walker, you must stay dormant until the poison has been completely flushed from your system and Josh has disposed of the poison, sterilized and sewn the wound shut," he said.

"I can't let her think I'm dead."

"You will until your body begins functioning and your blood flows completely blue and warms its self."

"I can't stand to hear her cry." I argued my reasoning flawed.

"Would you rather hear her cries of anguish if you were really dead, or for this short period of time?" Moon Dancer answered clutching me to him.

I relaxed back when I felt a sense of calm and heard the familiar voice.

Chapter EIGHTEEN

"Jace come here, hurry. What's happening to Kerry's arm?" Mom asked panicking as she watched the discoloration spread around the wolf bite.

"I've never seen anything like this, Mom," Jace answered rushing away slipping behind one of the curtains.

A moment later Josh came around the curtain; stood beside the table. His face etched in worry the moment he looked at the wolf bite.

"Mrs. McDaniels will you please go get Nakiya and ask her to bring me my healing bag."

"I will, but what's going on Josh?" she pleaded with fear filled eyes.

"I don't have time to explain. Please hurry," Josh insisted placing a clean towel under the infected arm.

"What's happening Josh?" Jace asked hurrying with a warm wash cloth to wipe away the cold sweat from Kerry's face.

"Something your modern medicine can't heal. The wolf bite injected a poison into him; the wolf was demon possessed. How's Shadow," Josh asked changing the subject wondering how he would explain this to Kerry's family when the doctor arrived.

"They're in trouble Josh; even with the stitches we've done those bite areas are to warm. Both have elevated fevers," Jace said feeling Kerry's brow. "I believe Kerry's body temperature has dropped, he feels so cold."

Sally and Nakiya entered the room followed by Danene. Danene even with her gut twisting fear for her little brother stayed back out of the way. Sally hurried over to Kerry and was alarmed when she felt the coldness of his skin. Nakiya now in her element had confidence in her shaman abilities walked over to Josh and handed him his medicine bag. She took her own medicine bag and opened it up taking out a wooden bowl and a small mallet for crushing herbs.

Looking into her brothers eyes Nakiya saw the dark intensity, and knew they was working with more than a mere wolf bite. Josh and Nakiya worked quickly and silently as a team. When Josh handed her the herbs she quickly measured the exact amount putting them in the bowl and chanted as she crushed the herbs blending them together.

Josh opened a small bottle and let the blue liquid flow into the bowl. Nakiya blended the fluid and the herbs together until it was the consistency of honey, and then handed the bowl to Josh. Sally grabbed his wrist.

"Are you sure this will work?" She asked her hand shaking even though she held his wrist.

"Something's can't be healed with modern medicine, Mrs. McDaniels. You have to trust me.

Slowly Sally released his wrist and walked around to the other side of the table her legs weak. Danene stepped up putting her arm around her mother's waist to help steady her.

"It will be okay Mom," she said looking at Josh for confirmation. "Come sit down and let them do what they do best. Dad and Doc are still a ways out and it has started to snow again."

Nakiya and Josh both stared to chant. Josh spread the mixture around the wolf bite and watched it turn a dark violet blue on Kerry's cold flesh.

Rob and Steve came from around the curtains hearing the chanting.

"What the hell is going on?" Steve walked aggressively over to his mother. His shoulders tight his brow lined. "I think we should wait for Dad and the doc, don't you Mom?"

Sally looked from Steve, to Rob and then to Jace. Steve walked over to the table his little brother was laying on and put his hand on Kerry's cold arm.

"He feels dead. What are you doing?" Steve shouted his mouth twisting.

Going for Josh's arm, Jace quickly reached up and stopped him.

"He knows what he is doing, Steve. Let him be," Jace spoke with conviction staring down his brother. He looked over to see if Rob was going to interfere. Rob shrugged his shoulders.

"I hope you're right Jace," Rob said with a harsh squint before he went back to the table that Shadow was lying on and pulled the curtain back around with one swift motion.

Sally watched Kerry's body jerk several times and raced to his side. Feeling his arm and his forehead she wept.

"Why is he so cold? He feels dead cold. He's not dead is he Josh?" she asked tears running down her face.

"No, he's not dead, Mrs. McDaniels, he just feels like it. I wouldn't lie to you," Josh assured her and continued chanting.

She backed away from the table shaking her head wanting to believe what Josh was saying. Brushing her hand across her forehead and moving in a daze she went behind the curtain where the two animals were being treated.

"How they doing?" she asked her mind foggy, she silently prayed for God's help.

"They're the same. I don't know how long they can keep this fever without it having an effect on their minds," Jace spoke barely above a whisper checking the IV's running in both of the animals.

"Brother Wolf's mate must be out of her mind with worry. I need to go find her something to eat."

"Mom I think you need to stay inside. That wolf will be alright," Rob stated putting his arm around his mother's shoulders.

"No, I have to go feed her," Sally responded and walked away from her son.

"Danene," Rob hesitated drawing in a breath.

"I'll go with her," she said stopping her mother from going outside without her coat. Helping her mother on with her coat, she also wrapped the scarf securely, partially covering her ears. After putting her own coat on they stepped outside into the cold snowy white world.

"I know what she's feeling."

"Who's feeling, Mom?" Danene asked putting her hand around her mother's arm guiding her back to the ranch house.

"Brother Wolf's mate of course," Sally said patting Danene's hand. We aren't the only ones worried about losing family."

"How can you worry about a wolf Mom, when my brother may be dying in there because of a wolf bite?" Danene said through clinched teeth.

"Danene, Brother Wolf tried to protect your brother. I cannot begrudge him or his mate for something they were not part of," she spoke as her tears froze to her cheeks. She sniffed and wiped away tear icicles from her face. "We need to trust Kerry to God's care along with Shadow and Brother Wolf."

After finding two venison roasts the two women took them to the tree line a short distance from the milking barn and tossed them into the trees. Not waiting, they hurried back to the vet hospital and watched for a few minutes from the porch. A short time passed before they saw the brown and white wolf crawl on her belly to receive the gifts.

"We are doing the best we can for your mate," Sally shouted her words into the falling snow hoping they would reach the female wolf and somehow she would understand. They turned toward the long drive hearing sleigh bells. "It's Jacob and Doc and someone else!" They stood outside waiting for the sleigh to come to a stop. Sally started crying again at the sight of her husband. She didn't focus on the third person with them as she hurried back inside with her hand in Jacobs and the others followed.

Doc quickly took off his hat and coat and picking back up his bag moved to the table that Kerry lay on.

"What's this?" He asked watching Josh and Nakiya chanting around Kerry's still body.

"You need to look at Kerry's leg, Doc. Josh is taking care of the wolf bite," Jace said with a pensive expression.

"Let me get his vitals before I look at his leg and I want to see that wolf bite myself," Doc said giving a dismissive glance at the others.

Sally clung to Jacob and the other boys left their stations and joined the circle around the table watching doc take out his stethoscope.

"Why is his body so cold? We need more blankets," Doc said harshly putting his instrument to Kerry's chest. He moved the flat round disc to several places before looking up.

"I'm not getting a heartbeat," he said his voice losing its power. Checking for a pulse on his neck there was still nothing. Doc hung his head.

"I'm sorry Sally, Jacob. We're too late."

Sally screamed and then sobbed into Jacobs's chest as he held her close to his body. Steve and Rob could have scorched the ground with the look they gave Jace and Josh. Danene fell heavily unto the chair by the door putting her face in her hands trying to hold back the screams going off in her head.

"Come on, let's go to the house and I'll put some coffee on," Jacob spoke, a numbness taking over his body. He pushed Doc's statement to the back of his mind not letting it register.

Sally turned back to Kerry and kissed him on the forehead.

"I love you son. I'll always love you," she cried feeling her insides shattering.

Jace watched as his family left and then looked up at Josh.

"He's not dead is he," he asked and turned to the cough he heard by the door.

"Harley Otter, how did you get here?" Josh asked going over to greet him putting his hands on Otter's forearms a warriors greeting.

"When I returned home my father told me I was needed here and I had to leave at once. He had filled my spare medicine bag with what he said I would need. I caught the train early last night."

"We haven't much time. I believe Kerry has shut down his vital organs to flush out the poison."

"Josh," Nakiya yelled. "Look at this." Nakiya said her mouth gaping open.

"A bucket Jace, one you won't miss. Hurry!"

Around the wolf bite a white slush started making its way out drawn by the herbs. In the bucket Jace procured, slush drops hit the bottom. It looked like angry green spiked worms.

"Don't let it touch you," Josh warned Nakiya.

"Here let me hold the bucket, I've got gloves," Jace stated taking Nakiya's hands off the bucket.

"Harley if you would look a Kerry's leg. He managed to drive a stick through it. By the look of the burnt flesh he did try to cauterize it."

When they heard the wolf howl it was only moments when they heard a gunshot. Josh stepped outside to see Jacob taking a rifle out of Steve's hands.

"This isn't going to bring him back, son. I promised Kerry we wouldn't shoot that wolf, and I won't break that promise. Now come inside."

Josh watched as Steve let go of the rifle and turn walking toward the hospital.

"He's coming here and he's in a foul mood."

"Lock the door until we're finished with this," Jace responded not taking his eyes off of the poison dropping into the metal bucket. It seems to have stopped. How will we know if all of it has come out?" he asked hearing Steve bang on the door demanding to be let in.

"Steve, go back to the house until you've cooled off," Jace shouted hearing some profanity and a few more pounds on the door.

Harley hadn't wasted time with what was going on but had prepared his poultice to wrap around Kerry's thigh. Nakiya went over to observe Shadow and Brother Wolf.

"When the herbs we put around the wound drop into the bucket you'll know that all the poison is out," Josh spoke getting ready the mixture to cleanse the wound before he sewed it shut.

"Then I believe it's all out. How are we going to get rid of these slimy things?"

"They need to be burned. Take them outside and torch them. Don't be surprised if we hear Shawgun again, as I believe those are a part of him as the wolf was."

"Kerry's skin color is returning to normal," Jace said excitedly.

"Then I think after I finish here Kerry's heart will start to pump his blood and his body will warm back up."

"Somehow Shadow and Brother Wolf are connected to Kerry, because their breathing isn't as strained," Nakiya related what she was seeing in the two animals.

"Well I guess I better get this done and have it over with. Perhaps with all the crying going on in the house if Shawgun does roar they might not hear it," Jace said as shiver went down his back before he put the matches in his pocket.

"Light it and back away in a hurry. You saw how the wolf lit up, Jace. You might want to keep an eye on the horses, also," Josh said walking back over to Kerry to start the final step to healing the bite.

"Josh, how did Kerry get himself in this mess?" Harley asked peeling the dead flesh away to where healthy pink tissue showed. "I'm glad he's out. This is a very painful procedure."

When he had removed the burnt flesh from both sides of Kerry's leg, Harley wrapped the poultice snuggly around the wounds.

"The inside has started to heal already. I have a few questions to ask him when he wakes up."

"You asked how he got himself in this mess. If you know Kerry at all, you know he lets his heart overrule his mind. And at this time with Shawgun out to kill him he can't afford to do that as you see what happens. Kerry is very vulnerable if he doesn't stay on task."

Josh was finishing the last stitch when they say the tower flame and heard the horrifying scream that sounded through the pines and timber not far away.

"Harley, my rifle is in the corner. Check on Jace and if you see a giant grizzly you have to aim for the heart or you won't stop him. And I don't know if that will kill him."

"Thanks for that last part," Harley said going out the door with the rifle.

Harley wasn't the only one outside with a rifle. Jacob and his sons come running with rifles in hand. Rob and Steve ran toward the horses in the corral hoping to sooth them before they broke down the fence. Before they reached the horses they had started to settle. Silence fell like a curtain. They were all hoping that meant the danger had stole away, however a cover of fear fell over those who had heard it.

Josh felt a pulse in Kerry's wrist and his body felt like it was warming as the blood started to pump through his veins.

Nakiya had snuggled carefully to Shadow not caring about his bloody coat but just for a feeling of safety. She smiled to herself after the tension lifted; knowing there was no way Shadow could have protected her in his condition.

"Nakiya, would you go and get Kerry's family and have them come back in here. He should be opening his eyes sometime this evening. But at least they'll know he's still alive."

"He's alive, he just called my name," Harley spoke out. "Weak. And he'll need more strength and courage to explain all this to his family," Harley said smiling and feeling thankful that Kerry's eight spirit animal showed up and he was very interested to know how it happened. To come through this injury it could only be 'one' with that much power.

******

The room expanded with love and concern. The warmth of my mother's hand as she laid it over my forearm gave me the desire to open my eyes. I heard voices of my family talking all at once and then go silent as Doc laid his stethoscope over my heart.

"I don't believe this and I don't know what you and your sister did?"

I assumed he was talking to Josh and Nakiya as I felt them still in the room.

"But I'm getting a heart beat. It's weak, however it's a pulse," Doc said lifting one eyebrow. "Let's have a look at that leg," he continued and pulled up the blanket exposing only the wound area. "What's this?" He asked sniffing the poultice wrapped around my leg.

"Please sir, do not remove that," Harley said putting his hand over the doctors to stop him.

I saw the fuzzy image shake his head and I presumed it was Doc as I tried to open my eyelids again. I felt my blanket start to slip to the floor and heard my mother gasp. She must have caught sight of the scars on my chest and side. Maybe I would wait until my blood flowed warm and my pulse returned to normal, which Snake said would when the sun went down.

"You'll have plenty of time to ask question Sally, when he wakes up but right now we should let him sleep."

I heard Doc say to my family and I really did agree. I had to come up with an explanation for my scars without lying to my parents and that would take me some time. After this Dad wouldn't let me off the ranch till I was fifty.

"*I think you are right there, Spirit Walker*," Moon Dancer agreed putting his chin on top of his clasped hands.

"*I believe Spirit Walker that the truth usually works the best. I agree your mother is lenient in more ways than your father because she is gifted in her physic abilities, some she isn't even aware of. Don't discount your father though, as he is only afraid of losing you. Talk with him. There is no other way to explain what has happened without being dishonest,*" Snake interjected.

348

"I guess you're right."

"I'm leaving now. You will recover fully with some added benefits. I will see you soon."

Snake said and faded away before I could ask what kind of benefits.

"I'm going back to sleep to conserve my energy, Spirit Walker." Moon Dancer yawned and disappeared.

I was getting use to this routine of being left on my own and I didn't like it any better than the first time.

"Shadow," I was hoping to get a response and not an angry one even though I did deserve it.

"I'm here Kerry," he responded weakly.

"How are you and Brother Wolf doing?"

"My wounds are healing as I'm sure Brother Wolfs are. It seems the stronger you get we do also. I feel that somehow now the three of us are linked together. Something I will need to ask Crow about. I suggest that you sleep." He said with affection in his tone.

"Harley, are you close by?" I reached out to my friend.

"It's good to hear you. It amazes me you have no difficulty getting yourself into trouble. I'm sure after we have disposed of Shawgun it will be quit a letdown as there will be no drama in your life," he said and I could feel him grinning.

"I liked my life before. What you might consider dull after this, will be fine with me," I responded back.

"You need sleep as I'm sure Moon Dancer has already told you. When you are stronger I want to know about your eighth spirit animal."

"Did you draw the poison out?" I asked thinking about Snake.

"No. Josh drew the poison out with the help of Nakiya. I took care of the puncture on your thigh.

"Harley tell them thank you for me."

"Kerry, I'll let you do that yourself when you wake up." Harley concluded and everything went silent.

I felt someone roll me to the side and a sleeping bag was pushed under me and then I felt someone put a pillow under my head. I would have rather been in my own bed but if by some chance Shadow and Brother Wolf were tied to me now and needed me close; it was a small price to pay.

We had escaped Shawgun's attempts to kill me and Moon Dancer, but only because of my friends. Without them we wouldn't have made it this far; and without Jace who believed in me carrying this burden would have taken more of a toll. I thanked the Great Spirit for my spirit animals that had protected me.

I didn't want to think about the coming weeks and the task still at hand nor the explanation I had to give to my parents. I just wanted to close my inner eyes and sleep.

The End of Book two